M. (François) Guizot

M. de Barante

M. (François) Guizot

M. de Barante

ISBN/EAN: 9783337031046

Printed in Europe, USA, Canada, Australia, Japan

Cover: Foto ©Raphael Reischuk / pixelio.de

More available books at **www.hansebooks.com**

M. DE BARANTE,

A MEMOIR,

BIOGRAPHICAL AND AUTOBIOGRAPHICAL.

BY M. GUIZOT,

TRANSLATED BY THE AUTHOR OF "JOHN HALIFAX, GENTLEMAN."

OMNIUM RECTA BREVISSIMA.

London:

MACMILLAN AND CO.

1867.

PREFACE.

It is scarcely necessary to write a Preface to this book. Its lifelike portrait of a true and great man, painted unconsciously by himself in his letters and autobiography, and retouched and completed by the tender hand of his surviving friend—the friend of a lifetime—is sure, I think, to be appreciated in England as it was in France, where it appeared in the *Revue des Deux Mondes*. Also, I believe every thoughtful mind will enjoy its clear reflections of French and European politics and history for the last seventy years, and the curious light thus thrown upon many present events and combinations of circumstances. For, as M. Guizot truly observes, " Les choses humaines changent plus à la surface qu'au fond."

In any case, there is something deeply interesting in the mere fact of this Memoir of a man of eighty-four, compiled by another nigh upon eighty—who with him has sailed through the same stormy seas, and writes as if he too felt already the calm and perfumed airs blown forward from the Invisible Land.

As to my translation, I will only say that it is as faithful as I can make it ; and that M. Guizot has done me the honour to revise it in passing through the press.

M. DE BARANTE.

On the 26th of November, 1866, a long procession, composed of public function- aries and simple citizens, rich men and poor men, tradespeople, labourers, and mechanics, together with relatives and friends, many of whom had come from a great distance, — in all more than eight thousand souls,—followed silently through a lengthy road, in cold and gloomy weather, a corpse which was being car- ried from the chateau of the village to the village church. One common sentiment animated all this multitude. Respect, af- fection, gratitude, sorrow, were written on every countenance, and audible in every

1866.

His funeral.

B

word, whether formal or spontaneous,
eloquent or homely, religious or merely
human, that was spoken beside this
grave. All paid with deep emotion their
sincere tribute to the departed, who had
long lived in the midst of them, and
was well known to every one.

Was he a man high in power, from
whom, till his death, his kindred and
friends, and these people who followed
him mournfully to his last dwelling, had
much to ask and to expect? Not at all.
For nearly twenty years he had lived
in retirement, having neither power nor
public duties; his only means of influence being his personal merits and private
virtues, the memories which linked him
with the past, his literary labours, and
his goodness of heart.

Was he a man who had carefully
sought popular favour; had made himself notorious on the opposition side of
public opinion: or tried to attract atten-

tion by flattering clever folk, and troubling himself to please the common crowd? Still less. All this homage was paid to one who had never adopted any but the most moderate and independent principles, which he had professed and practised whether they were in or out of favour with the government or the people; who had more than once sustained an unpopular cause, and remained faithful to it under the severest trials. It was in the highest and loneliest regions of thought that this dead man, thus accompanied to his tomb, had fixed his convictions, and drawn from thence the laws of his life.

We must seek for other reasons than ephemeral power, or the favour of the multitude, to account for the universal public sympathy which expended itself upon the coffin of M. de Barante.

The first and most apparent cause was, doubtless, the fame of his well-known mental superiority. He was one of the rarest spirits of his age. His intellect was at once lofty and flexible, solid and delicate, practical and refined; free-thinking, yet reverent and wise; capable of serious studies, yet alive to all literary and social enjoyments. It had been tested by the most opposite forms of brain-work: in politics as well as literature; in long labours of the pen, and rapid, lively conversation. To all these mental qualities was united a moral character upright, stedfast, faithful; independent without rudeness; most kindly and gentle at the core, though externally there was often a piquant mixture of exactingness and banter in both his words and opinions. It is the misfortune, often the fault, of great mental superiority, that it wounds those who contemplate its display, and excites even among indifferent people envy and dislike; but when, this superiority once established, its possessor gracefully abdicates all domination on that score;—when at last comes death, disarming it for ever in this world, and uplifting it to a higher sphere,—it regains all its rights and all its advantages, and finds once more not only the favour of the public, but the justice of the irritable and jealous-minded. As, even before his death, M. de Barante had found. Already he had reaped the reward of his many virtues; popular opinion had placed him in his just rank, and not a single recriminatory or even dissenting voice marred the sympathy which was poured out over his grave.

Still, not even this explains sufficiently the universal feeling manifested in France at the death of this good man : a feeling which attaches and will attach itself more and more to his memory. There is a still deeper cause, which ought to be recorded, because it sheds light upon our past, and gives hope for our future.

Born on the 10th of June, 1782, M. de Barante had witnessed and shared the seven successive *régimes* which have since been the lot of our country: the Ancient Monarchy; the Revolution; the First Republic; the First Empire; the Restoration; the Monarchy of 1830; the Second Republic; and the Second Empire. What events! What transformations in the intellectual, moral, social, and political condition of France! What destructions and reconstructions; what ruins and new creations! Above all, what trials and temptations for the men who were thrown on the current of such a boiling stream; what perils for both their principles and their virtue!

Trials have led the way to downfalls; temptations have made weaknesses painfully apparent; by the depth of reverses one can now measure the giddy heights of danger. Soon it will be a full century —three generations—during which both individuals and political parties have been a prey to changes, corruptions, and un- heard of difficulties in their opinions and their acts. Their deceptions have equalled their pretensions ; their cowardice has surpassed their rashness. Never has a grander spectacle been intermingled with scenes so ominous and so sad. Yet, in the midst of these contradictory vicis- situdes, and underneath this dark and foul fermentation, there has always existed in France, from the end of the eighteenth and during the course of the nineteenth century, one true and con- stant public feeling, secretly craving and striving after a permanent legitimate end. Under all *régimes*, and outside of all parties, there has been one party—that of good sense and morality : a party composed of honest men of moderate opinions, who desire to see all lawful rights respected, and look forward to the development, at once regular and free, of all the healthy forces of the human race. Ceaselessly battered down, deceived, led astray, hopeless, and apparently shattered, it existed still, and was continually renewing itself in spite of both its errors and its reverses, its failures and its discouragements : timid and unquiet, but honestly and perseveringly representing the national sentiment—the good cause— in the midst of all the theories and storms of European civilization. In the very heart of this party, M. de Barante was born, educated, lived, and died. He belonged to it, even from his cradle, by the traditions and habits of his family; he devoted himself to it, voluntarily, throughout his whole life.

His forefathers, whose surname was Brugière, were, about 1550, notable and wealthy merchants in the little town of Thiers, then a thriving place. In 1617, one Antoine Brugière bought the estate of Barante, and took its name, which

thenceforward became that of his descendants, who remained possessors of
this ever-increasing property.* They
grew into one of the most honourable
families in Auvergne, belonging to the
higher order of *bourgeoisie*, which, by its
agricultural or commercial labour, its
local functions, and its social and intellectual influence, was now taking in
France a position, as yet unacknow-
ledged by the State, and which, consequently, it was compelled to obtain for
itself, not by legitimate progress, but by
one violent effort, thereby causing the
most momentous social revolution in
history.

Once established in their territorial
domain, the ancestors of M. de Barante
renounced commerce, and gave themselves up to literary and scientific studies,

His father.

1782.

* Literally—*la métairie noble;* which means a
landed property, purchased from one of the *noblesse*,
and conveying with it some aristocratic rights and
privileges.

to local and magisterial duties, and to all
the occupations and interests natural to
men of settled fortunes and great intellectual activity.   His father—M. Claude
Ignace Brugière, Baron de Barante—
received all the liberal education possible
in his time, both collegiate and social.
The son thus writes of him, in family
reminiscences, which he has collected
with pious tenderness :—

*His
father's
youth.*

At sixteen my father's classical studies
ended.   He remained at Paris to take his
degree as a law student ; being then very
young and altogether free, but amenable to
reason, and filled with honest and high-
minded sentiments.   Neither the distractions
of society, nor the welcome that he received
in it, made him frivolous or lazy : on the
contrary, he acquired both the habit and
the need of intellectual pleasure ; together
with a strong distaste for vulgarity and
ignorance.   But his occupations wanted con-
secutiveness.   The manners of the time were
not favourable thereto.   Everywhere there
was a keen desire to know, to examine, to

judge; but mental cultivation was carried on more by means of the excitement of society than by study and meditation. My father was nevertheless one of the most earnest-minded men I ever knew. His great depth of feeling, as well as of conviction, could brook no shallowness of expression: indeed, it gave him sometimes a certain awkwardness and honest slowness which I think the worse of myself for not having inherited. Beyond all that he owed to natural temperament, to the true soul which God had endowed him with, and to his earliest domestic impressions, he was somewhat indebted to the social influences of his youth. He had had introductions to Oratorians and Genofevans— good Jansenists; and it was in parliamentary families that he had just been presented. The parliament of Paris was now exiled, and succeeded by what we call the parliament Maupeou. But the strength of parliamentary opinions and the hatred and contempt which all who shared them had for the despotism of the time, were remembrances vividly retained by my father. His recitals often made me seem to live in that gone-by period, when he must himself have been a vehement partisan, though I think he was no blind fanatic. But assuredly

His father's youth.

what he then witnessed exercised a strong influence over him, and contributed to give him a deep-rooted antipathy to the aristocratic despotism of the court.

*His
father's
marriage.*

After some years spent at Paris, M. de Barante (the elder) returned to Riom to assume the office of *lieutenant criminel du bailliage.** Soon afterwards he married. His wife, Mademoiselle Tassin de Villepion, came of an honourable family at Orleans. She had eight brothers and sisters, and only eighty thousand francs for her " *dot.*"

This marriage (writes her son), although it made them almost poor for the circle in which they lived, never gave my parents a single regret. Perhaps my father, having married a lady brought up in Paris, whose relatives were established there, was sometimes a little dissatisfied with his own inferior position ; but it would be a mistake to suppose that it caused either him or his wife any real vexation, or brought into their life the spirit of discontent. In those days society was so

* Anglicè —high bailiff.

regulated that ambitious tendencies were never sharpened by possible hopes ; neither his circumstances nor destiny could be easily changed by any man ; social position was not as now, subject to all the chances of fortune and accidental events. My father and mother enjoyed all the present blessings of their condition ; and if they ever wished for a different one, it was a desire so vague as never to affect their mode of life in the least.

Besides, there soon came to them an interest which absorbed all others, and became the one aim and occupation of their existence —almost their only thought. This was, their children. I can never recal without the deepest emotion, and an utterly voiceless gratitude, all that my parents did for me—all that I owe to their unexampled tenderness and care. As far as ever I can look back, I remember them, unceasingly occupied with me and my education ; seeking to develop both my heart and mind with a clear-eyed, rational, far-sighted affection. My mother suckled me herself, which was not the custom ; I never quitted her ; she watched over my earliest impressions, and I find in all of them no single idea which does not speak to me of her goodness and love—and my father's.

His father's children.

The education of youth was at that time a subject which occupied everybody's mind ; novel opinions were arising respecting it ; derived from the new philosophy under which everything was looked at from a fresh point of view. My father and mother, according to their individual peculiarities of temperament, directed all their thoughts and studies to this point, which was the constant topic of conversation among the men with whom they mixed in society. Consequently, I was the subject of incessant thought. Elementary books were continually manufactured and remanufactured for me. Everything was to be taught and explained to me by means of conversation. Walks, excursions, amusements, all were planned with a view to me. My father composed for me, a grammar made up out of Dumarsais, Duclos, and Condillac,— it has since been printed. I never read it now without being touched by the infinite patience with which he tried to reduce such abstract notions to the level of infantine intelligence ; and I marvel that he ever succeeded in so doing. Afterwards, my parents compiled a geography,—the dialogues which formed the introduction are written by my mother. She wrote much for us: tales, historical extracts,

carrying on for our benefit the education she
had received in her convent, and continually
learning in order to teach. Thus my early
studies progressed rapidly; and as my parents,
in spite of their love and anxiety for me, were
convinced of the indispensable necessity of a
public education, I was sent at nine years
old to the College of Effiat.

1820.

Here M. de Barante's youthful records
end. I must leap at once over twenty-
nine years—from 1791 to 1820.

A leap of 29 years.

He had lost his mother in 1801, his
father in 1814; yet, after all these years, I
find in the memorials written by his hand,
which he has left behind, the same respectful, grateful tenderness towards the
parents of whom he delights to speak :
their places, long vacant in the house,
are never empty in his heart ; their son
seems still to hold them living, close,
and dear.

My father (he says) was only fifty-eight
when we lost him ; an age which warranted
us in hoping we should long enjoy his affection ; and he had wholly contented himself

throughout life in household love. I think it was the loss of my mother and brothers which broke his heart, and finally gave him his death-stroke. To him I owe everything. All that is of most worth in me comes from him. Every year we spent together, every misfortune we shared, drew us closer and closer. We became like two friends—two old friends, who had the same remembrances, the same griefs. Upon all subjects we understood one another with half a word. Besides natural affection, he had a kind of fancy for me—for my personal society, for all that I said and all that I wrote. Whenever we happened to be separated, we did not let a week pass without writing to one another; confiding mutually our sentiments and mental impressions. His somewhat restless, reserved disposition, and my habit, for which he often blamed me, of letting my mind work within itself, thereby losing the natural *abandon* of youth, ended by our settling into complete harmony, so that nothing troubled our delight in being together.

To this day I am conscious of having a ceaseless crowd of thoughts, reflections, and fugitive sensations, with which my father alone could have sympathised; which are bound up

with our long intercourse, and which I no
longer know what to do with. Sometimes
there come to me words, which I am obliged
to force back into silence, because it is to him
only that I would have cared to address
them; him only they would have interested,
or won from him an amused smile.

No one but myself ever thoroughly knew
my father, and all that he was worth, in heart
and brain. One of my keenest regrets, and
I think he shared it, though silently, was
that, during his lifetime, he was scarcely
enough appreciated. He passed in the world
for a man of excellent good sense, some learning and capacity, and a great deal of merit;
but if he had had less of timid self-distrust, or
a position of more prominent activity, if he
had been encouraged and animated by success,
he would have far better demonstrated what
he really was. After the blow which struck
him in the midst of his career, he lost courage.
He had absorbed himself in his domestic
affections, renouncing both energy and emula-
tion; and then he lost the one special happiness for which he had given up all other. In
this thought, which had long grown habitual
to him, he wrote, almost in his last days, " I
hoped to have augmented the heritage of

The son's estimate of his father.

C

honour which I have to transmit to my children." Of that heritage he certainly diminished nothing; nay, he left his family in
higher repute, more important, and well-
established, than it had been before his day.
Whatever he owed to his ancestors, we owe
still more to him. It is as a legacy to my own
children that I write these remembrances of
my father. If I in my turn transmit to them
the paternal heritage, perhaps with some addi-
tions, they will understand that I owe entirely
to the affectionate lessons, and, above all, to
the example of my parents, the success which
has attended me in my long career.

The son's debt to his father, and legacy to his children.

I know of only one writer, Montaigne,
who expresses himself towards his friend,
La Boétie, in terms so touching, and with
a tenderness so close and sweet. And
what strikes me most, is not merely the
filial love of M. de Barante, and the respect, at once modest and free, in which
he holds his father, but the deep belief
which they both have in family ties and
family rights—the entire family, as belonging to the past, the present, and the

future. Each is occupied by what he owes to his ancestors and his descendants: honouring the one, and desiring to be honoured by the other. Each lives, as it were, in the graves of those whom he has never known, and by the cradles of those whom he will never see. There is no sentiment more noble and disinterested than this:—none which, while belonging exclusively to humanity, attests more strongly the dignity of human nature—its lofty records and still loftier hopes.

I now quit the family aspect with regard to M. de Barante. He presents himself to me under another and a totally different view. However great for him, as for his father, was the charm of domestic life, he did not shut himself up within it: he had instincts, tastes, and faculties which required wider gratifications. When very young, he had thrown himself into public life, and taken

*His father
in prison.*

part in its interests and impressions, at
first most painfully and pitifully.   For
when scarcely ten years old, he had seen
the daily life of his family upset : his
father arrested, imprisoned, and menaced
with the Revolutionary tribunal.

I was sometimes admitted to the prison
(writes he)—but more often repulsed, with
severity.   To give some pretext to my visits,
I used to carry vegetables ; and as I was
always searched, I had to hide in an artichoke
the letters which were to be given to my
father.   Many a time I heard sung under
the prison windows—

> " Il faut du sang—il faut du sang
> Pour affermir la république."

Once it came into my head to draw up a
petition and present it to a member of the
Committee of Public Safety, whom I had
sometimes seen among my father's ac-
quaintances ; he treated me as a mere child,
and called me his little friend.   This, and the
smile and tone which accompanied the reply,
offended me deeply.   I was indignant that
any man should not receive seriously the
entreaty of a son for his father's liberation.

The events of the 9th Thermidor,* together with the indefatigable devotion
and presence of mind of Madame de
Barante, saved her husband. Afterwards, when people began a little to
believe in the restoration of social order,
the Commissary of the Convention in
Auvergne appointed M. de Barante to
the office of Procureur-Syndic of the district of Thiers. Of this his son writes:

Nothing was farther from my father's mind
than the desire to throw himself at such a time
into public affairs, but his friends and all the
most honourable citizens of Thiers pressed
him to accept the office. To assist in establishing order and peace in his own district; to
calm restless minds, and make a truce between
opposing parties, appeasing the rancour of
the one, and reassuring the other against a
threatened reaction—this seemed an honourable duty, in which he was encouraged by the
kindly trust placed in him by all honest
people. My father yielded.

His father in office.

* The downfall of Robespierre.

Later still, in the glorious early days of the Consulate, the first Consul Bonaparte had desired his colleague, M. Lebrun, to draw up a list, out of which he could select names for the various *préfectures,* which had been newly instituted.

One day M. Lebrun was dictating this list to M. Creuzé, his private secretary, and a great friend of my father's and mine, young as I was. The Consul could recollect no name for the department of l'Indre. M. Creuzé asked leave to suggest a name, and gave my father's. " I don't know him," said the Consul, " but set him down ; I will think over it." So the name remained on the list, and my father was made a *préfet :* but he was appointed to l'Aude, not l'Indre, which suited better a friend of M. Lebrun's.

My father went to thank the Consul Lebrun, who received him graciously. " Monsieur," said he, " I have done on your account a rash thing ; I have chosen for an important post a man of whom I know absolutely nothing ; but I do not regret ; all that I hear of you convinces me that I have done wisely. Possibly, you may be a trifle too aristocratic, but that is not bad, in moderation. You will not be shocked if young girls like better to dance on Sunday than on Decadi.* I trust to your prudence and discernment."

Thus a political career opened to M. de Barante the father, in which he was soon to be followed by his son. The young M. Prosper was, however, then preparing himself for a different vocation by other studies: he had gone through the curriculum of the Ecole Polytechnique.

At school. Politics against mathematics.

But (says he) in my second year there I found I had less taste than ever for mathematical sciences. They should have been my principal occupation, for they lie at the root of all the studies which I had to follow; but I neglected them, and expended all my ardour upon natural sciences, physics, mineralogy, chemistry. Besides, the aspect of public affairs, and the progress of government, had inspired me with a strong wish for a political career. Before quitting Paris to visit my parents at Carcassonne, I had gone through my examinations in order to enter the mining department at the school. I had acquitted

* Alluding to the revolutionary change in the calendar.

myself well enough in all the studies I liked, but very badly in mathematics, so I was uncertain if I should pass or not. I explained this to my parents, and they received favourably my idea of devoting myself to the public service—indeed said they should have advised it themselves.

So it was agreed that on my return to Paris I should take steps to enter the Foreign Office, a career much to my mother's liking ; but until I begun it, I was to remain at the Ecole Polytechnique, resume my studies there, and continue them until I found other work. However, I rebelled against this prudent plan. I hated my school, where I found myself inferior in everything that there it was most important to know. I foolishly ran away from the Ecole Polytechnique, and hid the fact from my parents. My Paris friends had received me well, and flattered me with hopes of soon getting into the Foreign Office. I believed them, and allowed my father to suppose I was at school still. Soon, all was discovered, and I was overwhelmed with shame at this, the heaviest fault of my life, and one which even now I cannot recal without amazement mingled with bitter regret. Still, I had not misused the liberty I so unfairly gave

myself. I led a studious and solitary life
with one of my friends. I read incessantly,
and I learnt English.

After his mother's death, and to dis-
tract his father a little from this heavy
grief, the two took together a short
journey through the middle and south
of France.

1801.
*His
mother's
death.*

We stayed some days at Barante, a spot to
us full of tender memories. This visit worked
in my mind a sort of revolution; it seems to
me now as if every serious thought I have
ever had, every moral and religious conviction, dates from this time. I learnt the true
value of things; my conscience became clearer
and more severe. I read much in a book, my
father's favourite, which had hitherto irritated
rather than humbled me, *Les Pensées de
Pascal.* It left a strong impression on my
mind.

On our return to Paris we gave up any
thought of the Foreign Office. M. Chaptal,
then Minister of the Interior, received my
father well. I was fellow-lodger and friend of
his son: he wished to take me into his own
department, in order to prepare me for future

1802.
*The
Foreign
Office.*

administrative duties. So, in 1802, I was admitted there as a supernumerary. My father went home with my young sister, and I remained alone in Paris.

For a long time after then I was profoundly sad at heart, with a strong liking for solitude. In the Ecole Polytechnique I had learnt one thing—a great distaste for frivolous drawing-room society. I enjoyed reading serious books, begun of my own accord to study law, tried to get general notions of administration in the midst of the dull routine work of my office ; and I followed with intense interest the course of public affairs. We corresponded incessantly, my father and I. He lived on, sad and solitary, discharging the duties of his préfecture, until an unforeseen event intervened to break the even tenor of his days.

The Concordat,* concluded in 1801, and promulgated solemnly in April, 1802, was little in harmony with the predominant opinions and habits of the nation. The First Consul, according to his usual ways, did not press the point, but left the country time to accustom itself to the changes he had ventured

---

* A treaty with the Pope, Pius VII. re-establishing the Gallican Church.

upon. The bishops were not installed until quite the close of the year. But in spite of all this delay and precaution, it was a critical moment. Everywhere people rebelled against this restoration of ecclesiastical authority. In some towns there were even riots. At Carcassonne, the disturbance was so great that stones were thrown, and the priest was attacked and wounded before the very altar.

My father had never exercised his authority with harshness and violence, but he showed now great firmness; he did not shrink from the riot, and immediately commenced pursuit against those who had originated it. The revolutionary party rose up in arms against him, and sent messengers to Paris, where their influence among the subordinate officers of government was much greater than that of the *préfet*. The First Consul in this case, as in many others, threw the blame on the unsuccessful side. Many *préfets* were dismissed, either for having been too weak, or too severe, in the suppression of the riots. This happened to my father. But as he wrote me daily word of the state of things, I was enabled to communicate with M. Chaptal, who, being very well disposed towards him, took his part with the First

1802.

His father as préfet.

Consul. Finally, Bonaparte's dictum was— "Well, send M. de Barante to Geneva; he will get on well with the Protestants."

This was not only a signal promotion for the *préfet*, but became for his son the foundation of many ties which influenced M. Prosper de Barante's mind and character during his whole career.

Geneva (writes he) is not at all like a provincial town, imitating vulgarly and conceitedly the manners of Paris; its better class is formed of people who are both rich and cultivated. The many visits of strangers to Geneva, and of the Genevese to other countries, have mixed them up with the European aristocracy, and imparted to them a certain tone of good manners; they are always *comme il faut*, if not always quite at their ease. The town is a centre of intelligence, as well as of wealth and piety. One may associate there with clever and enlightened men who, finding themselves at liberty and on their own estates, are estimated at their just value, and neither fettered nor choked up, as often happens in provincial life. In the midst of such a society my father took his place, better appreciated than he had ever been before ; respected, and paid attention to, both for his own sake, and on account of his position ; since each day, the magistrates of the place, like the government of whose power they were the representatives, gained more influence and importance.

The older inhabitants of Geneva, in spite of their keen opposition to the imperial *régime*, felt the merit of their new *préfet*, and were grateful accordingly. M. Sismondi writes thus—on the 9th of January, 1809—to the Comtesse d'Albany, the widow of the last of the Stuarts, and also of the poet Alfieri :—

We are fortunate in having among us now a perfect model of an honest, good man. M. de Barante, our *préfet*, tries by all means in his power to soften the misery which Government scatters abroad everywhere. He compensates for the evil which he is forced to do by the good he does of his own will. He knows how to make himself beloved even while enforcing conscriptions and levying taxes. We feel that his probity, gentleness, justice, and the perfect order which he has established in all things that depend upon himself, save us daily from countless vexations, and allow us to suffer from no other misfortunes than those which are inevitable.

His father's friends and his own.

Such associations were for young Prosper de Barante, who spent a portion of each year at Geneva with his father, a solid advantage as well as a keen delight. Soon he discovered still greater pleasures. At Coppet, near Geneva, on the boundary line of France and Switzerland, lived M. Necker, and his daughter, Madame de Stael, who were the objects of eager curiosity to every Swiss traveller, and the permanent centre of an ever-renewed and ever-changing circle, composed of the *élite* of European society.

M. de Barante thus writes in his reminiscences of that year :—

M. Necker was then an old man, in feeble health, and his very secluded life rendered him an object of veneration, even to those

who were most hostile to his political opinions.
It was his society that my father most enjoyed.
Madame de Stael's conversation was attractive, but there was in it something more vivid,
rapid, and bold, than suited the character of
my father's mind; he had never been accustomed to see the most fugitive impressions
translated into language as strong and vehement as if it were meant to express passionate
emotions and deeply thought-out ideas.

1810.
*Madame
de Stael
and the
circle at
Coppet.*

This was natural. A man of mature
age and timid nature, and moreover a
wise, responsible Government official,
was sure to find himself a little uneasy
in the company of such an impulsive
being—impetuous both in thoughts and
words ; but for other standers-by this was
precisely what gave to the society and
conversation of Madame de Stael so
wonderful a charm and power. Her
intellect and her imagination seemed
perpetually seething, in a whirlpool as
wide as it was full : her mind was
always fermenting within and boiling

over, on all occasions, and upon all
sorts of subjects. What a fascination
must this have been to a young man
of rare capacity, fresh and unsophisti-
cated, whose life had hitherto been shut
up between his own home and the
Ecole Polytechnique—domestic interests
and solitary studies! Into what a new
world—and rich as new—did Madame
de Stael cause him to enter! And at
the same time, while she came forward
to him full-handed, laden with treasure,
there stood beside her this old man,
her father, venerable and venerated, one
of the most notable actors in the French
Revolution, who now serenely scattered
around him all the memories and all
the lessons of the past which, during
his long life, he himself had purchased
so dearly.

These two persons, and their differing
eloquence of character and words, the
vistas they opened up to him, both

before and behind, could not fail to
exert over M. Prosper de Barante that
potent charm which results in the influence of close intimacy. The prudent
solicitude of his father was roused
into anxiety for his son's future, since
the dislike and even malevolence of the
Emperor Napoleon to Madame de Stael
placed not only herself but her friends in
a position that was always painful and
precarious. Young Prosper de Barante,
while keenly enjoying this friendship,
as brilliant as it was sweet, had no
idea of sacrificing his whole life to it.
Still it could not fail to influence his
character, ideas, and sentiments in a
manner that was afterwards demonstrated in a wider and less generous
circle than the little society at Coppet.

In 1805 the French Academy proposed as the subject of the prize of
eloquence, *Tableau Littéraire de la
France au dix-huitième Siècle.* For four

D

1805.
*The French
Academy
prize.*

successive years was it given, without producing any work that the Academy deemed worthy of a prize. In 1810, however, the prize was awarded to two of the competitors, MM. Jay and Victorin Fabre; and that the merits of both might be recognised, the Comte de Montalivet, then Minister of the Interior, doubled it. Meantime, the young supernumerary in the Home Department had been among the competitors; but the essay of M. Prosper de Barante found no favour with the Academy. Instead of delivering it, he had it published. This was in 1808, before the prize had been decreed to his two more fortunate rivals. However, after their success, their work was quite forgotten; while that of M. de Barante has gone through seven editions, and is still often given as a prize volume at *lycées* and colleges.

The depth of thought in this book has contributed to its lasting success as

1808.
*His first
book.*

much as its brilliancy of talent. It is
a bold, novel step in a new intellectual
road. Its author does not treat French
literature of the eighteenth century
solely in a literary point of view. He
takes it in its influence over the social
and political condition of France—her
faiths, her manners and customs; the
whole active moral life of the nation :
and this influence he defines and appre-
ciates with firm independence. There
is in his book both a certain reaction
against the recent past, and a passionate
impulse of thought towards the dawn-
ing future of his country. The young
nineteenth century was beginning to free
itself from the shackles of the eighteenth,
and, criticising its progenitors without dis-
owning them, was assuming a character
of its own, natural and free. It was
precisely this cause which excited in
the French Academy of that date a
feeling of spleen against the work of

a young, unknown writer; and when
the book was published, M. Garat, a
talented Academician, but a credulous
and stedfast disciple of the eighteenth
century, expressed this sentiment sharply
enough.

But the public did not share it.
Though influential still, the eighteenth
century had ceased to be the fashion :
liberty of speech and opinion was allowed concerning it, and a taste for novel
views in both literature and philosophy
began to prevail more and more every
day, even among most opposite parties.
Madame de Stael had lately published
her work, *Sur la Littérature considérée
dans ses rapports avec l'état moral et
politique des nations*, and M. Bonald
was developing brilliantly his doctrine
" that literature is the expression of
society, and that upon it rests the responsibility of the faults and misfortunes
of a nation." Therefore this book of M.

de Barante, which bore the impress of a strong instinctive respect for law and order, combined with great freedom of thought, and was written in a style at once piquant and natural, and animated without being declamatory, earned at once for its author a distinguished rank in the new school of philosophy and literature which was then arising — awakened by the course of modern events and the turn of modern minds.

A change of position now befel the young man. He grew weary of being a supernumerary clerk in the ministry of the Interior, and though well aware how much it would cost him to be no longer able to pass a great deal of his time with his father, and with the dear society at Coppet, he applied for the appointment of Auditor of the Council of State, which in 1806 he obtained.*

*1806.
He becomes celebrated as a writer.*

He applies for an auditorship in the Council of State.

* The "*auditeurs*" were young apprentices—so to speak, in the Government offices, and reporters on questions that came before the Council.

1806.

*He attends
the Council
of State.*

I reached Paris (he says) at the moment
when the Imperial Government, drunk with
the glory of the victory of Austerlitz, burst
forth in all its splendour, and tried to domineer
over Europe. I was well content with my
new appointment. It gave me position,
regular occupation, and the hope of proving
that I had sense and brains ; but what pleased
me most was the opportunity it offered of
frequently seeing and hearing the Emperor.
Not that I was inclined to feel for him the
blind adoration shown by those about him ;
but the desire to know him and judge him
fairly, to appreciate his forcible character and
high intelligence, to find out what he was and
what he was not, had long been my constant
thought. The sittings of the Council of State
were, therefore, for me, a sort of drama, in
which I listened with ardent curiosity to
actors and speakers, and above all to the
Emperor.

*Discussion
concerning
the Jews.*

The first discussion at which I was present
was eminently interesting. In returning from
Austerlitz, the Emperor had stopped at Stras-
bourg ; he there heard many complaints
against the Jews. Popular opinion had up-
risen vehemently against the usury they practised. A great number of landed proprietors

and farmers were burthened with enormous debts, leaving behind claims for sums far beyond those which had been lent to them. It was said that more than half of the land in Alsatia was mortgaged to the Jews. The Emperor promised to set right these great abuses, and arrived in Paris with a conviction that such a state of things could no longer be tolerated. He laid the question before the Council of State. At first it was carried to the Ministry of the Interior. M. Regnault de St. Jean d'Angely, the president, commissioned M. Molé, a young aspirant in the department, to report in the affair. To politicians and lawyers the matter seemed clear enough; undoubtedly no legal authority could recognise any difference between citizens on account of their differing religions ; to inquire the creed of a creditor, in order to determine his right to be paid, was, according to both the letter and spirit of French law, an idea as foreign to both public opinion and public custom as it was to legal precedent. But, to the great surprise of the Council, M. Molé produced a report, which concluded by urging the necessity of making the Jews subject to exceptional laws, at least concerning transactions of usury.

M. Molé's report on the Jews.

I arrived in Paris some days after the sitting of the section in which this report had been read, and heard how it had been received with smiling contempt by the State Councillors, who saw in it merely a clever literary article. belonging to the anti-philosophic school of M. de Fontanes and M. de Bonald. M. Molé, however, was in no wise disconcerted; there had as yet been no discussion, the question requiring to be carried before the whole Council. M. Regnault exposed it summarily, scarcely thinking it necessary to assert an opinion that was universal. But M. Beugnot, who had just been made Councillor of State, thought this a good opportunity for his *début*, and handled the question from its very root with much good sense and cleverness; so that he won everybody over to his side. The President then stated that the Emperor, who attached great importance to this matter, held opinions differing from those which seemed to prevail in the Council; the discussion must, therefore, stand over till a day when his Majesty could preside in person.

This took place at St. Cloud. M. Beugnot, who then for the first time spoke in the Emperor's presence, and whom his late success had a little intoxicated, was this time

emphatic, pretentious, declamatory; everything that a man ought not to be at a Council
of State, where the discussion is simply a
conversation between men of business, who
require neither deep research, nor grand
phraseology, nor dramatic effect. The Emperor plainly grew impatient, especially at a
ridiculous phrase used by M. Beugnot, in
which he had entitled this exceptional
measure against the Jews, "a battle lost on
the field of justice." On the termination of
the speech, his Majesty replied to it with
extraordinary energy and vivacity, employing
both seriousness and raillery, speaking against
theories and absolute general principles; and
still more strongly against men with whom
facts counted for nothing, and who sacrificed
realities for mere abstractions. He caught
up severely the unhappy phrase about "a lost
battle," and getting more and more animated,
ended by actually swearing, a thing which, to
my knowledge, he had never done before in
any Privy Council. Finally, he concluded by
saying, "I know that the author of the report
is not of my opinion; I wish to hear him."

Then M. Molé rose and read his report:
M. Regnault courageously defended the
popular opinion, and even that of M. Beug-

Inquiry concerning the Jews.

The Jews are legally recognised in the State.

not. M. de Ségur also risked a few words, saying that he did not see what could be done.

His Majesty calmed down, and the Council terminated by deciding upon an inquiry into the condition of the Jews of Alsatia, their principles and practice as concerned usury. The commission was composed of three *Maîtres des Requêtes*, M. Portalis, M. Pasquier, and M. Molé, who were appointed to that office on purpose. *Préfets* were charged to point out any Rabbins or other Jews of importance, who might give information to the commission, which information was to be received by M. Pasquier. Now, for the first time, something was definitively learnt concerning the Hebrew nation, their division into sects, their hierarchies, laws, and customs.

M. Pasquier's report was most instructive. Even the Emperor was quieted down by it, and came to the sensible opinion that the Jewish worship ought to be officially recognised, and assume a legal existence. After the report of the commission, and in order to satisfy the people of Alsatia, an imperial decree was made, establishing some transitory articles of law, and a sort of registration, which

1806.

in future kept all Jewish creditors within the
limits of the common law of France. Then,
in order to regulate the exercise of the
Jewish worship, a grand Sanhedrim was
summoned, the result of which was, that
this matter, begun in a moment of irritation
and of malevolent intolerance, ended by
a solemn recognition of rabbins, syna-
gogues, and the civil equality of the Jewish
people.

Some months after, when the Emperor was
in Poland, seeing the eagerness of the Jews
to be of use to the French army, and their
readiness to serve without fee, as spies or
contractors for the commissariat, he said,
laughing, " See the benefit I have got out
of the grand Sanhedrim ! "

M. de Barante was shortly afterwards
called to join in scenes more striking
even than that of a great man exer-
cising a rough but powerful influence
over all his Ministers. During the cam-
paigns of 1806 and 1807, and as a result
of the battles of Jena, Eylau, and Friedland, a number of young *auditeurs* were

He is sent abroad with the army.

sent out to Germany and Poland, to administer justice, under the very cannon's mouth, in the provinces occupied by our armies. M. Barante was one of these. He has left behind him many records of his painful mission. Without any historical pretensions, they are full of those minute, precise, and vivid details which are the life and soul of history. I cannot resist giving some extracts—so characteristic of the events of this brilliant epoch and of the actors therein, by whom these events were guided. These extracts are remarkable, not only for the vivid impressions which he received, but for the clear, stedfast judgment which the young man, a modest spectator, had formed on all that passed around him.

His arrival at Berlin. I arrived at Berlin (he says) on the 8th November, 1806. Our orders of departure placed us under the command of M. Daru, Paymaster-General of the Army. At his

house I first presented myself. I knew him a
little, and we had various mutual friends.
He received me kindly. I found him very
busy; surrounded by *commissaires* and *or-
donnateurs*; receiving every minute officers
sent from each regiment in the army for money
or supplies. Conversation was brief and to
the point. He told me he had no power in
appointing our destination; the Emperor
decided that himself; and then he asked me
to dinner. This day his guests were the
deputies sent to the Emperor by the Duke
of Brunswick, requesting that he might
remain in Brunswick, and live there till his
death. These deputies, as was well known,
had been harshly received; consequently no
Generals nor higher officials paid them much
attention. It happened that I knew one of
them, Baron de Sartoris, a Genevese, and
the Duke's Chamberlain; so I placed myself
beside him at table. His other neighbour
was General Chasseloup, with whom he had
a little conversation, chiefly concerning the
fears entertained by the inhabitants of Brunswick.

"Ours is a poor country," said he; "the
French will find little in it; they will soon
have eaten everything up."

"Well," replied General Chasseloup, "when we have eaten up everything, we will eat up *you*."

These kind of manners were a novelty to me, and impressed me with dislike as well as regret. I felt that our army would leave behind it hatred and rancour among the whole German population, and I feared both the instability of a power thus misused, and the vengeance which might be taken upon us, one day. M. Daru, absorbed as he was in military affairs, wherein he had such an important part to play, did not altogether forget his common sense or his pleasantry. I found him one morning musing in the Botanical Gardens at Berlin. "I am going to commit a grand act of barbarism," said he. "I came here to see if the orangeries and conservatories could be turned into stables. The thought continually pursues me, that if the allied armies of Europe should invade France and enter Paris, their military comptroller, seeing the galleries of the Louvre, may consider what a magnificent hospital it would make, and count up how many beds he can place there !"

Six weeks later, towards the end of

December, the Emperor quitted Warsaw, in order to place himself at the head of the army, and pursue the war.

M. de Barante continues :—

Commissariat and military officials of all sorts, ambulances, &c., were still stuck in the mud on the route. M. Daru knew not how to provide for the wants of the troops who had entered on the campaign without anything being settled beforehand. A battle was impending. The wounded would be, in a few hours, brought back to Warsaw, where there was no hospital ready to receive them. Every available assistance was summoned ; and in default of military commissaries M. de Canouville and myself were ordered each to provide an extempore hospital. Time pressed. We already heard the booming of cannon. The theatre of war was only a few leagues distant. The wounded would probably arrive in the course of the night.

He is ordered to make an extempore hospital.

I had orders to provide myself with everything necessary at the cost of the municipality of Warsaw. I found among these officials complete goodwill, and even a kindly eagerness to help. They showed me many grand mansions which might be used as hospitals.

I chose one which had once been very splendid,
but was now deserted and dismantled. The
ceilings of the vast saloons and long galleries
were still covered with paint and gilding,
many apartments being most elegantly decorated. But now my business was simply
to furnish my hospital.

*How he
executes his
orders.*

The municipality put under my orders a
working man who went from street to street
collecting beds, mattresses, linen : which were
taken from every householder, and which I
saw piled upon carts. I did not enter the
houses myself, and escaped all the rigours and
unpleasantness of the task ; but I insisted on
its rapid execution. The day was advancing
—there was not a minute to lose ; night came,
and still I had not a fragment of earthen-
ware necessary for the use of a hospital. The
municipality gave me an order upon a potter
in the place to provide me with whatever I
desired ; and then one of the Jews, who
swarmed about the town offering or selling
their services, was charged to conduct me to
the pottery-works. The command had been
given hastily and roughly. The Jew did not
comprehend it, and dared not ask questions.
We started, and after having wandered about
for more than an hour through streets half

lighted, or not lighted at all, he, seeing my impatience, said to me in German—of which I understood very little—that he had no idea where he was ordered to take me!

We went back at once, and I explained the mistake; upon which the Polish commissary fell upon the poor Jew,—beat him furiously, dashed him to the ground, and trampled him under foot. Such was the way in which both Poles and French treated this luckless race, who patiently bore all sorts of brutalities, waiting opportunity to make money, by causing their enemies to pay dearly enough when they paid at all, and by buying very cheaply from the soldiers things which had cost them nothing.

When my hospital was ready, just before night-fall, I went to inform M. Daru, stating that I now required only surgeons and nurses. He had none, and sent me again to the municipality, who supplied me as before. Towards evening on the next day, the wounded began to arrive, and I continued to fulfil scrupulously and compassionately my sad duty. These unfortunate soldiers could not explain their sufferings to the surgeons, who knew not a word of French. Some had their limbs so shattered that amputation was

Hospital miseries.

E

urgent : there were no instruments at hand, and the municipality could furnish none. I have still before my eyes a grenadier, handsome, and manly-looking, but deadly pale.

"Monsieur," said he to me, "they ought to cut my leg off ; gangrene is beginning there— it is already quite blue. Just look!" He turned down the coverlet and showed me the bare, bleeding limb. "I know well," he added, "after we are wounded nobody heeds us nor takes any trouble concerning us. We are no longer of use—we are only a burthen ; they would rather we were all dead. Let them kill us, and there will be an end of it."

The peace of Tilsit. In July, 1807, peace being made at Tilsit with both Russia and Prussia, M. de Barante, who then held an appointment in Silesia, thought he had come to the end of his labours.

We *auditeurs* hastened to get our accounts in order and lay them before M. Daru : we wished not a day's delay in returning to France, for we longed to quit the scene of our unpleasant duties. It did not occur to us that peace had brought no change in the condition of Prussia, which must still be governed as a conquered country. But on arriving at Berlin I recognised this, for I found all things on exactly the same footing as eight months before : a French administration, Frenchmen at the head of financial affairs, and M. Daru the real ruler of Prussia. I had been desired to bring to him our Silesian accounts. I did so, inquiring what hour next day I should submit them to him, with the necessary explanations.

"Oh," said he to me, "you will give us a great deal of money."

"Very little," I replied, "only two or three millions (of francs) ; the rest has been made up by forced levies."

"There will be disputes concerning these. I have not approved of them"

"There is not one which does not rest upon either the Emperor's orders or your own decision," said I.

"Yes, but I do not always explain myself clearly. I am liable to be cheated. Listen," added he, taking a more serious tone; "I do not wish to give you false reasons. The Emperor left me the other day at Konigsberg. In getting into his carriage he said, ' You will remain here with the army: you will feed it and supply it, and bring me back a sum of two hundred millions.' I exclaimed against this. 'One hundred and fifty, then,' said he, shutting the carriage door, and driving off without waiting my reply. So you see, that Prussia owes still one hundred and fifty millions, and my accounts will prove it. We know well enough how to find arguments and calculations in order to demonstrate this. Spare me them at least for to-day."

I answered, that it was not I who should have to dispute this matter with the people of Silesia, or be perplexed by hearing them accuse us of our broken promises, since the Emperor had appointed me *sous-préfet* of Bressuire. It was no advancement certainly, but I did not complain ; it removed me from these parts. I was about to present myself at my new post.

"All right," said M. Daru, "I expected you would take the matter thus."

I had, in fact, as soon as I arrived at Berlin, read in the *Moniteur* my nomination to this petty *sous-préfecture*. My colleagues considered it a disgraceful thing, and declared that letters in which I had spoken somewhat too freely of the miseries of war, and the condition of these conquered countries, had been opened. For me, I asked no explanations of anybody, and retracted nothing. Bressuire was a village which civil war had reduced to a population of five or six hundred. It was situated in the interior of Bocage, fifteen leagues from any high road. I began to consider whether I ought not to give up a career where I was kept in an inferior position, and made the sport of malevolent interferences; whether, in short, I ought not to send in my resignation.

He did not do this; nor had he any cause to do it. One of his letters from Silesia had indeed been opened by Government. "It had appeared imprudent," said he afterwards, " but it had given not a bad idea of my judgment or of my opinions." Many of his colleagues had also been nominated *sous-préfets*, and M. Regnault de Saint-Jean d'Angely continued to show towards him an earnest and active kindliness.

He advised me to present myself before the Emperor, who was then at Fontainebleau. But, although I was reassured on many points,

1807.

His relations with Government.

regarding which my nomination to Bressuire had caused me apprehension, I wished to run no risk of hearing unpleasant words, and therefore I did not take his advice.

The young man was right. He was not the one to accept meekly the harshness of a despot : it was wiser to present himself at his post without delay.

It is only twenty leagues (he writes) from Poitiers to Bressuire, yet it took me three days to arrive there by carriage : the roads were as bad as those of Poland. Imagine first, twelve leagues of level plain, that is to say, of mud ; then eight leagues of thick ' forest, or of a road hollowed out between two hedges. Sometimes I had to hire horses, sometimes oxen. Often I got overturned, or broke the carriage poles, and twice I had to sleep in village public-houses. At length, on the 25th of December, 1807, I made my entry into Bressuire, about eleven in the forenoon.

The aspect of the place startled me. Houses in ruin, covered with ivy and nettles ; here and there hovels built among the rubbish. I went down a whole street without finding

one decent dwelling. The first I came to
was that of the Receiver of the *arrondisse-
ment*, where I was to stop. He offered me
an arrangement which suited me, and in a
quarter of an hour we had settled everything.
I took his house : the rooms he let to me
were few and ill-furnished, the walls being not
even papered, and the office of the *sous-
préfecture* was at the other end of the town ;
which, however, was not distant.

Some days after my installation I wrote to
my father thus :—" I will tell you nothing bad
of Bressuire. I like it better and better, without, however, attaching myself to it strongly.
For the people, I have never seen worthier
folk—simple, moral, religious, and apparently
devoid of what is so common among our small
provincial towns, the spirit of envy and malevolence. Crimes are rare : out of six law-
suits, five end by a mutual settlement. Manners
are of a higher character than ordinary. The
life led here is one of extreme simplicity, the
women dressing much more plainly than the
servants in great houses ; they do all cookery,
and continually rise from table to wait upon us.
Nobody knows anything of what is passing
in the world without. We talk of hunting ;
we joke with the awkward riders ; we make a

little harmless fun of Monsieur le Curé, respecting him sincerely all the while. After dinner we sing old songs, and dance round dances, while the men tell stories which have descended from generation to generation since the time of Rabelais. I cannot easily put myself into this merry mood ; and am content with being, if not popular, at least respected.

What a strange change of society for a young man who had lived in the *salons* and enjoyed the intimate friendship of Madame de Stael; who had been present at Imperial State Councils, and followed the Grand Army through its victories. But M. de Barante had received a solid education : he had a deep sense of duty, a taste for study, a keen spirit of observation, and that disposition of mind, laborious, wise, and gentle, which, without effort, knows how to take patiently life's small trials, and to profit by the most trivial advantages.

I think (wrote he to his father) that I shall succeed well in this administration ; it is easy

1808.

Letters to his father.

enough. Above all, to insure peace and obedience, it is advisable to try no police measures: there is no rational ground for them. The Nonconformist priests are perfectly quiet, and are without any influence on the refractory conscripts. I have even been told that when they see public functionaries respectful towards religion, they submit at once, and rejoin the Established clergy. There is not, in the whole district, a single person under surveillance. The war in La Vendée has not left behind one gentleman who took part in it. The only important proprietor here is M. de la Roche-Jacquelein, brother of the Vendéen hero, and husband of Madame de Lescure, the widow of another noted officer. He is rich, and people have tried to prejudice me against him, but he took no part in the war of La Vendée, being at the time in St. Domingo in the English army. He has few connexions in Paris, and scarcely ever goes there. He receives little society in his house at Clisson; his chateau was burnt down and destroyed, and he has since made habitable a sort of dwelling erected on cleared land. He is much beloved by the neighbours, and in his relation with them has no aristocratic ways of any sort.

At Bressuire, as at Geneva, M. de Barante followed his natural instincts. All his tastes were refined and delicate; all his feelings generous and high; whenever and wherever he found the same in others, he and they amalgamated as surely as flame ascends and water rises to its own level. The opinions and social habits of M. and Madame de la Roche - Jacquelein were certainly very different from those of M. Necker and Madame de Stael; but there was the same lofty and pure moral atmosphere— the same spontaneous tendency towards all that was noble in the soul and in life.

I soon formed (writes he) a most sincere friendship with Madame de la Roche Jacquelein: I went constantly to the Château de Clisson, where I was received with cordial kindness. There I conceived the first idea of writing the memoirs of Madame de la Roche-Jacquelein. Ever since my arrival in the country I had intended to write a history of the war in La Vendée. She had began her memoirs, the first chapters of which were already written; these she put into my hands, with some notes which she had made on the subject. She guided me in my researches. She introduced me to several Vendéen officers; I got them to recount what they had done or witnessed, and she herself, with a truthful charm which she was not able to reproduce in her writing, related to me everything that had fallen under her own observation, and all she had suffered,—describing likewise the deeds and characters of those whom she had tenderly loved and lost in the war. I visited all the places she indicated, and got the peasants to show me the battle-fields, in order thereby to make more vivid to my own mind the events which I had to describe, and the men whose characters I wished to draw. Consequently, when I took pen in hand, it seemed no more a mere literary exercise; I wrote simply the truth, according to the impression which it had made upon my mind.

This is the strong characteristic of M. de Barante's *Memoires de Madame de la Roche-Jacquelein:* a narrative at once rich and simple; personal, without pretension; eloquent, not rhetorical; pic-

1808.

His first idea of the Memoires de Madame de la Roche-Jacquelein.

turesque and vividly coloured, without betraying too much art; full of descriptions and minute details, which vivify rather than retard the book. Evidently the narrator has taken in his work the same deep interest with which he inspires his readers. It is a short historical epic, as written by a companion of the hero.

He completes and republishes his first book.
At this time, in what he called his "hermitage" at Bressuire, M. de Barante completed his *Tableau Littéraire de la France au Dix-huitième Siècle*, a work long planned, and, after its failure in gaining the Academy prize, published in a more mature and extended form than he had at first intended.

Restless ambition is not the only ambition which succeeds, and sometimes prudent and honourable conduct bears its fruits, without any trouble being taken concerning it. The Emperor Napoleon was in the habit of observing men closely, and knew how to make use of those whose talents and character he respected, even though he did not altogether reckon upon their enthusiastic and complete docility to himself.

In the month of August, 1808 (writes M. de Barante), the Emperor, in crossing the department of Deux-Sèvres, stopped at Niort. I went thither to meet him. He asked me many questions, almost all relating to the Vendéens, and appeared satisfied with my replies. He was aware that I had been successful in my present office, and I asked nothing from him. M. Maret, who accompanied him, gave him to read my *Tableau Littéraire de la France au Dix-huitième Siècle,* which had just appeared. I suspect he had already read it; but after having fluttered the leaves about a little, he said to M. Maret, "We must make the man a *préfet."* However, on my return to Bressuire in December, 1808, I still felt that in spite of appearances the Emperor had some ill-will towards me. I thought I would take my own course of action and send in my resignation, when I learnt that on the 13th February, 1809, I had been appointed *préfet* of La Vendée.

A short time afterwards I went to Paris,

and M. Maret there told me what the Emperor had said to him.

"I have two important nominations to make," said he; "I want a private secretary and a *préfet* of La Vendée. Show me two young men, both capable and reliable."

M. Maret replied, that among the young officials he knew, M.M. Mounier and Barante appeared to him most worthy of trust.

The Emperor reflected a little. "Well, well," said he, "then Mounier for myself, and Barante for La Vendée."

I was then twenty-six years old. Certainly I had advanced pretty fast in my career, without having once sacrificed either a principle or a friendship.

The Imperial choice was good, and time proved this. M. de Barante administered justice calmly, mildly, free from any rough assumption of rule, and from murmurings among those whom he ruled; executing his instructions, often difficult and painful, so as to gain both the Emperor's approval and the gratitude of the people.

But it was from a higher Hand than

man's that he received his best reward,
for at this time he contracted the union
which formed the happiness of his long
life, and filled his last days with the
infinite consolations of pious tenderness.
Towards the end of 1811, he married *His*
Mademoiselle Césarine d'Houdetot, the *marriage.*
sister of one of his most intimate friends.
She was very beautiful; not rich, but
well-born and well-connected; as sweet
to live with as she was charming to
behold. To her he owed the pleasantest
satisfactions of the outside world, and,
within their own, the purest domestic joys.

Early in 1813, M. de Barante obtained
leave to visit Paris, his wife being there
awaiting the birth of her first child.

I was invited (he says in a letter) to one of
the Empress's *soirées.* These assemblies were
not crowded—there was not even official
costume required: everybody being in ordinary
dress. We entered the *salon :* — then the
Emperor and Empress quitted their apartments, said a few words in passing to the

guests: immediately afterwards, all went to hear an act of an Italian opera represented on a moveable theatre placed in a neighbouring *salon.*

I was accosted by M. de Fontanes, an agreeable conversationalist, who hated Italian music. After the opera we returned to the Empress's *salon,* where was served a small supper, she sitting at table with a few important personages. Those who had not this honour were summoned to another *salon.* M. de Fontanes and myself, stuck fast in the doorway between the two apartments, went on chatting together. The Emperor, who did not take supper, quitted the first *salon,* stopped, and began conversing with us—or, in order to be more exact in my recital, he began by asking abruptly, " What are you talking about ?"

M. de Fontanes answered politely, " I was speaking to M. de Barante of an article on Bossuet which he has inserted in the *Biographic Universelle,* and which well deserves all the success it has obtained."

Said the Emperor to me—" Have you not made a book against Voltaire ?"

" Sire, upon Voltaire," I answered.

" Yes—yes," said he; " I know you are very impartial."

M. de Fontanes, accustomed to his ways, gave him a clever answer. He liked to be thus comprehended and responded to by people of talent : a few words, shewing that one felt interest and pleasure in listening to him, put him on his mettle. He excelled in catching at once the tone of mind and character of those over whom he wished to have influence.

At first he spoke to us about the project which he had of confiding the future regency to the Empress, saying that such a power ought to be trusted to no other person, as none other than a mother could possibly be so entirely and safely devoted to a royal child. He cited, as instances of this, the mother of St. Louis, and Anne of Austria, mother of Louis XIV.

The Emperor upon Louis XIV.

"For," said he, "Mazarin was only a councillor; the real authority lay with the Queen-Regent."

From the minority of Louis XIV. he passed to discussing his reign, and gave us a fine panegyric on that monarch. "He was a man in earnest, and had a true feeling for the dignity and honour of France. He also was the creator of a working executive. He had fine armies, and gained grand victories; he was able to resist all Europe. He and not Henri IV. gave to France the pre-eminence which we still maintain."

The Emperor here did justice to an objection which I ventured to make, in behalf of Henri IV., and, correcting his own rather too hasty judgment, began to speak about that king and his high qualities, both as a general and a politician, but always with a certain tone of superiority ; adding, "His life was an unhappy one ; he deserved better things." Then he went back upon the whole career of Henri IV.

"In his youth, compelled to an unwilling marriage ; almost massacred at St. Bartholomew ; constrained to change his religion ; held captive in a court which longed for his destruction ; the head of a rebellious and undisciplined party ; conquering his crown at the sword's point ; reigning in the midst of conspiracies and assassins ; betrayed by his mistresses ; worried by a cross-grained wife, and slain at last by the stab of a poignard."

Here the Emperor stopped for a moment, then continued—

"I compare sometimes his lot with mine. The crown was his by right, yet with what difficulty did he obtain it ! He reigned, a good and able sovereign, and he was assassinated! Whilst I, not born to a throne, have ascended one simply and naturally, without any serious difficulty, and am able to sustain myself there in peace, fearing no peril. It is because I am the mere creation of circumstance, with which I have always marched along, hand in hand."

In listening to these remarkable words, I could not help asking myself whether the Emperor really maintained this marvellous tranquillity of mind, after having lost an army of five hundred thousand men, and having still to fight the whole of Europe without one probable chance of success?

It is impossible for me now to recal how he passed on from Henri IV. to Cæsar and Alexander; but he did so, and we heard him silently. He approved of Cæsar as a general and great soldier, but he thought little of him as a political ruler.

The Emperor upon Cæsar and Alexander.

"He aimed too much at pleasing the people, and therefore could never attain to any real power."

But for Alexander, the Emperor's admiration was without any critical reservations.

"Kingdoms conquered; cities founded; distant expeditions undertaken; new dynasties

established in Asia; his memory left in
each of the three known quarters of the
globe. He was a great man."

In hearing the Emperor speak thus, we
recognised the impulses which had led
Napoleon to Moscow.

Meantime, supper was over; the Empress
had passed into the second *salon*; the
Emperor saw she was tired of waiting so
long, and he quitted us.

He is appointed préfet of La Loire Inférieure. Some weeks after this conversation,
Napoleon appointed M. de Barante
préfet of La Loire Inférieure: a high position, and a great token of Imperial esteem.
He would be still placed in the region of
the civil wars of the west, but he exchanged the smallest town for the largest,
and had the citizens of Nantes to govern,
instead of the peasants of Bressuire.
While he recognised the Emperor's
favour, M. de Barante was far from
rejoicing therein. He wrote thus to
his wife, in telling her of his departure
for Napoleonville :—

I am saddened: saddened and deeply

touched by all the farewells that I receive here. The grief that our departure causes is incomprehensible; it really surprises me. Every one meets me with tears in his eyes, and the hardest and most indifferent are weak as children. This feeling, which honours while at the same time it keenly affects me, seems to extend everywhere, and among all classes. The other day at Luçon, during the sitting of the commission for augmenting the conscription, I heard people whisper, "Never had we among us a man so just." It was a sweet recompense for everything. I assure you, my dearest, it is hard to quit people who love me so well. I ought to have asked permission to remain here; alleging I was sure to be more useful than I could be elsewhere. The other day, I was reading that the early bishops scrupled always to remove from one church to another, counting it a sort of spiritual adultery. And, truly, if I had asked to be removed from Bressuire, or taken any steps of myself in this matter, I should have felt very much ashamed. I shall not easily find again such kindness, such trust; a town of sixty thousand inhabitants is not the place in which to be known and appreciated. Here, in La Vendée, I have daily news of everybody: peasant or artisan finds my door continually open; I have leisure to talk with him, and take an interest in his affairs. But at Nantes I shall be forced to act the official, and I shall soon grow like all the other *préfets* in France, instead of being the ideal *préfet* which I had imagined in my youth.

His new post.

M. de Barante was right in regretting his modest appointment in La Vendée. But to Nantes he carried the same spirit of wisdom and gentleness, affectionate equity towards those whom he ruled, and open-eyed, honest, candid loyalty towards Government. Nevertheless, his post in the Loire Inférieure from 1813 to 1814, was a difficult and painful one. It was the last year of peril and struggle of the Imperial *régime;* of its indefinite exigencies and too well foreseen reverses; of the endless, measureless sufferings and sacrifices which it then imposed upon France. The prudent moderation of one single *préfet* was powerless to breast

the current, even as all the severity
of the central government, and all the
victories of its Imperial master failed
to rise above it.

And M. de Barante was engaged in
this fatal movement without any illusions
of his own, with no strong passions, and
with a clearness of vision, which dated
far back, and which he owed to the high
tone of his character and his constant and
imperturbable rectitude of judgment, as
much as to his liberal, acute, and observant
mind. I will extract from his notes only
two examples of his prophetic wisdom
concerning the events in which he was a
sharer, and the fiery genius of the man
who originated them. I take these examples, not out of the last days of M. de
Barante's administrative career, when the
sinister light of impending consequences
was already glaring upon all eyes, but at
the outset of his public life, and from the
impressions made on the young *auditeur*

of Silesia, and the obscure *sous-préfet* of Bressuire, by the then splendours of the Empire.

He says, at the first of these epochs :

His impressions of the Emperor.

The ten months which I have spent in Germany, either at the theatre of war, or at least in the region conquered and occupied by our armies, have left on my mind ineffaceable records. Undoubtedly the sight of the calamities and miseries of war—the sufferings of the conquerors, as well as the conquered, must produce on a mere spectator—who, having run no danger, has no right not to be pitiful—a vivid impression ; but if he confines himself to this sympathetic feeling, and dwells upon it, he will merely repeat commonplace facts which every war carried on by such and such a general, at such and such a time, must inspire. In this sense, the Emperor was quite right in writing to M. Maret, " Plan with M. Daru how to dismiss from Warsaw those useless government-clerks, who are only losing their time, and who, unaccustomed to the events of war, write back to Paris stupid nonsense about it." Nevertheless, putting sensibility aside, one may draw from what one has seen in Germany and Poland instructive political lessons, which make one comprehend the character and genius of the Emperor, as well as conjecture his probable future.

Thus, his campaign undertaken after the battle of Jena, and his invasion of Russia at the beginning of winter, without any fixed plan, without any formal intention to re-establish Poland, nor even much belief that Poland could be re-established ; the dispersion of our army on the left bank of the Vistula, without forecasting the march of the enemy's army ; then the sudden concentration of our forces at Warsaw, without preparations of any sort, without magazines of stores ; his beginning a campaign at the end of December, and carrying on a war in the mud, without the slightest appearance of success, three weeks after the attack upon the snow, at the imminent risk of being frozen and starved to death ; all this, forgetful of Austria, whose vengeance and self-interest were sure to profit by the chance, and Germany, left free to raise her head again—such things could not but forcibly strike an observer. The question in point was not the event, successful or otherwise, of a scheme falsely conceived, and badly calculated, but the mad impulse born of his passion for war and adventure, his restless necessity of doing something, with or without purpose, trusting to his own ability; which ability consisted in seizing on any chance in which there was a hope of success, and making the most of it. This was what every one knew and perceived—nay, a few said it out plainly, and even before the time when the Emperor, by his bold resolve not to repass the Vistula, but to try and recompose what remained of his superb army during the winter, laid the foundation for the victory of Friedland and the treaty of Tilsit.

But the boldness and strength of his will, and his capacity for executing it, do not justify his political conception of this war. So much imprudence, such important interests rashly staked, could not fail to leave in all men's minds great inquietude concerning the future. There was nothing stable in the conditions of peace ; they were evidently merely a point of departure from whence to proceed to new adventures. Russian power placed in relation to and on an equal footing with the power of France, to the suppression of all intermediate sovereignties, was the presage of an immediate war. Prussia, reduced one-half, trampled under foot, insulted in the person of her sovereign, and in the honour of her army, occupied

in a military capacity during peace, would
necessarily exalt herself into patriotism, and
a desire for vengeance. Austria, exasperated,
would be eager to try once more the opportunity in which she had failed. Germany,
where the victor was establishing a French
kingdom, would doubtless seek to form herself
into a national unity.

But the most obvious sign of an ominous
future, was not so much the state of mind of
entire Europe, as of that of the man who had
subjugated it ; a mind whose vocation was
obviously to establish nothing solid and
lasting. Forgetful of the true interests of
France, clever doubtless in instituting order
and regularity in the administration of his
empire, but always occupied in preparing projects of war and conquest, he is for ever
proposing immense and chimerical schemes,
less in the hope of realizing them than because
they afford employment to his indomitable
activity, carried away by the impulse and
habit of warlike feelings. His marvellous
faculty of command, his quickness and cer-
tainty of observation, the keenness of his
intellect, and, above all, the grand argument
of success, had caused those around him, those
who were dragged by him into movement and

1814. action, to forget the thoughts they had about him three months before. But it was impossible this should be the case with those who did not live under the close shadow of his influence, and who had leisure to observe him without being disturbed in their reflections concerning him.

How the Legitimists felt on the matter. In France, whether by the bulletins of the Grand Army, or through the notes of the *Moniteur*, the war appeared under an aureole of glory. But the ancient friends of liberty still maintained their own opinions and their own doubts. The few partisans of the legitimate Bourbons preserved their old aversion, and regarded the Empire as a phase of revolution : they knew not how to criticise or to predict anything. But the mass of the nation at large was filled with pride at the dazzling grandeur of France, and conceived a sincere admiration for the Emperor ; yet even they began to detest a war, of the termination of which they instinctively despaired.

Some months later the young politician of Silesia carried to his obscure *sous-préfecture* of Bressuire the same opinions as these, given with the same impartial frankness. As I have already stated,

he had met there a family—rich and respected landowners, faithful Legitimists,
but still living tranquilly, strangers to
all underhand, treasonable practices, and
disposed to be on a good understanding
with all the honest functionaries of the
Empire.

There was soon (says M. de Barante) perfect confidence between Monsieur and Madame
La Roche-Jacquelein and myself. Madame
de Donissan, mother of Madame de la Roche-
Jacquelein, lived with them; she had been
lady of honour to Madame Victoire, daughter
of Louis XV. and had resided at Versailles,
where her daughter was brought up. Both
were faithful to their old associations, and
yet very reasonable; they regretted bitterly
the past, but spoke freely of the errors which
had led us to the Revolution: while they
honoured the king, queen, and princes, they
were not silent respecting the various scandals,
which they declared calumny had greatly
exaggerated. These ladies had no thought
of attaching themselves to the present *régime;*
they wished, though without much hope, that
it might not last. I remember saying to them

one day—" I believe, as you do, that the
Emperor is destined to ruin himself; he is
intoxicated by his victories, and his con-
tinual success. A day will come, when he
will attempt the impossible—and fail. Then
you will see the Bourbons back again. But
they understand France so little, they will
make so many blunders, that they will bring
on a new revolution."

The fall of the Empire. To one whose judgment had long
been so free and so clear, the fall of
the Empire and the restoration of 1814
could have been nothing strange or unforeseen. M. de Barante accepted both
at once as necessary events, and also
as a promise of liberty and peace for
France, now exhausted and compromised by absolute autocracy and by constant war. Being without news of Paris
for some days, he waited anxiously the
issue of the crisis, solely occupied with
maintaining, at Nantes and the department, public order, and some sort of
agreement between the various local
authorities.

The Vendéens (says he) gave me much anxious thought. I feared lest they might make some attempt which would rekindle civil war. Until now they had remained quiet both in town and country, a certain number being enrolled, registered, and armed ready for action if summoned. Without knowing what was preparing, I knew their friends, and had little doubt of their projects. On the other hand, I was aware of the state of public feeling at Nantes ; the townsfolk had no love for the Imperial *régime*. The ruin of their commerce, and the sacrifices which had been imposed upon them to maintain the war, had brought them into a condition of habitual discontent. Still they disliked the Vendéens, whose resistance had caused them many sufferings. The greater part of the gentry were watched with restless malevolence ; and had they attempted any rising, the whole town would have also risen to suppress it.

Such was the condition of affairs when the courier arrived from Paris. I had long reflected on what I ought to do in such a crisis, which it was easy to foresee would come ; I had considered it as regarded my personal opinions, but still more with a view to the interest of the district, the government of which had been confided to me. There, above all, lay my duty. One false step, and there might have broken out a civil war, which, above all things, I wished to prevent.

His conduct on the fall of the Empire.

As soon as the courier appeared, a great crowd thronged the post-office : it would have been impossible to bring me my despatches ; they would have been snatched from the clerk in charge of them. I went to the post-office with General Brouard, commanding officer of the department. I knew his opinions were opposed to mine, and that he was quite capable of refusing obedience to the Provisional Government, which had just proclaimed the Bourbons. I made him understand that the Empire was in fact at an end ; that Napoleon had abdicated, and the Grand Army existed no more ; that, in short, the recal of the Bourbons was the only chance of concluding a peace a little less fatal to France. The General did not reply. His grief and annoyance were plain enough. When I saw him a little more resigned, I said to him, "All the town is out there, impatient for news. Shall we go and give them some ?"

So we went out together to the top of the flight of steps ; and I read aloud the proclamation of the Provisional Government, which

1814.

was very well received by the crowd. Then
I proposed to the General to come with me
to the theatre, and repeat the same thing.
This displeased him—everything displeased
him—but he agreed. At the theatre the news
was received in the same quiet manner. I
heard some murmurs here and there, but they
were lost in the general satisfaction. I quitted
the theatre ; it was nine o'clock at night ; the
town of Nantes was tranquil, and the towns-
people seemed even happy to see the end of
a state of things which had been full of de-
plorable and almost insupportable anxiety.

The restoration changed in no degree
the position of M. de Barante. He
received neither marked favour, nor
rapid advancement. He asked nothing
from the Bourbons; no more than he had
asked from the Emperor Napoleon; and
he remained simply *préfet* of Nantes.
His nature was more high-minded than
ambitious, and in his conduct there
was less of pushing hardihood than of
dignified reserve. Besides, although
still young, he was already among the

His position with the new Government.

G

number of those who, in face of startling events, are, whether approving or disapproving, neither dazzled nor intimidated by them, but view them in their various aspects with an equal eye, maintaining a firm independence of thought and action.

M. de Barante did not hide from himself either the mournfulness or the peril of the present public crisis, or the errors and weaknesses of the restored Government. However, taking it as a whole, the new state of things pleased him, both as a man and a citizen. War and despotism had been exchanged for liberty and peace. In the restoration there was a great mingling of the ancient and the modern, tradition and innovation ; union, if not unity, was established between the divers classes of the nation ; the principles of 1789 were consecrated by legal charter ; constitutional monarchy, with its roots settled in history, and its victorious

modern liberalism, had at last begun.
There was much to fear, but also much
to hope. M. de Barante was among
those in whom hope overcame fear,
and who anticipated a happy future for
the new *régime.*

So when Napoleon returned from
Elba to try his last venture—an act
on his part the most heroic and most
egotistic, as it was the most fatal one
for France—M. de Barante, grieved as
he was, did not hesitate an instant,
but sent in his resignation of the *préfecture,* and testified openly, though sor-
rowfully, his opposition to the Emperor.
The return of Louis XVIII. had found
him well-disposed, but not ardent in the
Legitimate cause ; but the Hundred
Days made of him a staunch royalist.

As such, he was soon called upon to
act towards his party with the same
independent foresight that he had shown
while he held office under the Imperial

Government. The Empire of the Hundred Days had fallen; a reaction, violent but natural, had brought the elections (for the *Chambre des Députés*) in harmony with the events of the time; the *Chambre* of 1815 had met: a position of affairs quite novel, and unknown since 1789, suddenly appeared. In a victory, not of their own gaining, the party hostile to both the revolution and the Empire had now the ascendant: more than this, they had in their hands all the weapons of war for the new combat now impending; for they had possessed themselves of the institutions and strength of the representative *régime* and of political liberty. They used these weapons boldly; took haughtily all the consequences of so doing, expecting that victory would result in power. But a higher fact, proved by all that has happened in France and in Europe for the last twenty-five years, appeared to

oppose both their pretensions and their
hopes. Of itself alone this party in
France was very small, as feeble a
minority as that of the Protestants at
the end of the sixteenth century, when
after forty years of civil war Henri IV.
became king.

During that monarch's days of struggle,
the Protestants had been his faithful
companions and devoted champions, had
bravely fought and cruelly suffered for
his sake, and thought they had a right
to triumph and reign with him. But
Henri IV. was a Protestant no longer.
He believed, and his most acute friends
and most necessary allies believed with
him, that in order to become a king
he must become a Catholic. He made
his decision, and quitted the ranks of
the religious minority to enter those of
the national majority. After such an
act he could not, ought not to govern,
except in accordance with his new

position. By the Edict of Nantes he assured to the Protestants some share of liberty, as much as the exigences of the time allowed, and which he sincerely wished to guarantee to them; but power belonged essentially to the Catholic party. On this condition solely could France escape from civil war, and find—as she did find indeed —prosperity, social progress, order, and peace.

The parallel between Henri IV. and Louis XVIII.

Generations come and go, but human affairs change more on the surface than beneath, more in appearance than in reality. The political questions of the eighteenth century had replaced the religious disputes of the sixteenth; but the situation of Louis XVIII. after the promulgation of the Charter, was almost identical with that of Henri IV. after his conversion to Catholicism. The majority, the immense majority, were evidently attracted to the principles of

1789, and to the essential results of the Revolution. Louis XVIII. in twice entering France, charter in hand, had placed himself in the ranks of this majority : he could now only govern with it and by means of it. Therein was, for the French nation, both might and right; for the King of France, necessity, and his royal oath.

A large proportion of the sincere adherents of the House of Bourbon believed that such was the position of affairs; they therefore accepted and resolved to carry out, in concert with Louis XVIII. and his ministers, the political course which the time demanded. M. de Barante was from the first among these. While regretting the schism among the Royalists, he kept up resolutely the contest which it occasioned. From 1815 to 1820, whether in his two offices as privy-councillor and superintendent of casual revenue, or else as

*He is
summoned
to the
Chamber
of Peers.*

member, first of the Chamber of Deputies, to which he was elected in 1815 by
the departments of Puy-de-Dôme and of
La Loire Inférieure, and then of the
Chamber of Peers, to which the king
summoned him in 1819, he persevered
steadily in this line of conduct. The
questions concerning the life-tenure of
judges' appointments, recruiting, the
press, elections, and finance affairs, all
of which were mooted at this period,
furnished him with an opportunity for
speeches which, without producing a
great effect at the time, were remarked,
and remained remarkable, as models of
political skill and moderation, in the
very heat of political warfare.

In the Parliamentary arena M. de
Barante was neither a close and impetuous debater, nor a ready and vigor-
ous orator; but he had great exactness
and loftiness of thought, careful pre-
cision of language, and a safe instinct

for seizing upon generous sentiments, and upholding them as the country's truest need. And when in 1820 the divisions in the ranks of the Royalists widened more and more, when amongst the moderate party, which until now had held power, some, more ambitious for their country, or more exacting in their own opinions, expressed aloud their objections to the cabinet of which the Duc de Richelieu was head, and were, by means of M. de Serre, then Keeper of the Seals, removed from the Privy Council; then M. de Barante, less strong in the opposition than they, but as faithful to his individual friends as he was to his general opinions, was, with M. Royer-Collard, M. Camille Jordan, and myself, included in that measure, which was as sad for those who carried it as for those who submitted to it, but inevitable to both. The Duc de Richelieu's cabinet, and his political creed, were not sufficient, we believed, to found the government which we all had it in our hearts to establish ; and nevertheless, neither the present position of the Crown, nor that of the parties in either Chamber, made it advisable to summon any other cabinet in opposition to the Duc de Richelieu and his policy. M. de Barante, accordingly, refused the post of Minister at Copenhagen, which was offered him as a sort of compensation ; not wishing, in a common disgrace, to be treated otherwise than his friends.

He begins a new epoch of activity. Thus began, for him as for me, a new epoch of influential activity ; and I think, for both of us, one of the most busy and happy periods of our lives. We were out of all political office and responsibility ;— not that politics were become indifferent to us ; nay, they held a large place in our thoughts, and we sometimes threw ourselves into them with an honest and hearty opposition, which, however, was neither hostile nor factious; but this opposition absorbed wholly neither our time nor our minds. Free and pure intellectual activity— literature, philosophy, home and foreign history—became our chosen occupation, and formed the source of our social sympathies, as well as our link with the general public, in whom our principles and our books excited, and fed, an earnest curiosity.

It is the high privilege of literature, that during periods while political liberty sleeps, intellectual freedom may still flourish—alone indeed, but still powerful enough to elevate men's minds, unite them in noble pleasures, and satisfy at least a great part of their human nature. The Augustan age and that of Louis XIV. are, to use conventional language, speci- mens of this outburst of literary life in the absence of political life; but the age of Pericles, of the Medici, and still

His intellectual career.

more modern epochs in France and England prove that the struggles of political freedom may be perfectly reconciled with a crisis of literary splendour, and with the progress of the human mind, disengaged from any other thought than the pursuit of the good and the true.

French literature from 1820 to 1830.

The combination of political liberty and literary activity always has this effect : it gives to the writings of the period a character wider, more virile, more stamped with wholesome reality. Thus, under the Restoration, in the ten years between 1820 and 1830, when the men who had mixed in political life were removed from it, they, without ceasing to call for and to use their rights therein, carried into literary labours the activity of their natures. The younger generation, still animated by a strong political spirit, entered upon the same path with all their enthusiasm and force of intellect. Literature under every form — poetry, philosophy, criticism, history — gained thereby, both in extent and variety of thought, and in the bold search after simple truth, without detriment to original and ideal aspirations.

In this general mental progression it was to history and foreign literature that M. de Barante's inclination tended. His translation of Schiller's dramatic works, and his History of the Dukes of Burgundy, date from this period. Both possess this remarkable characteristic, that while they exhibit clearly the new lines of thought into which were passing both historical studies and literary criticism, they are stamped with an originality, without effort or one-sidedness, which attests both the writer's judicious independence, and his flexibility of thought and impression. He warmly admired the dramatic works of Shakspere and Schiller, on whose canvas arge and free, nature is painted with

so bold a hand, while human life
and society are sounded to their lowest
depth, and represented in all their
various elements and forms. He noticed with great sagacity the essential
difference between what is called the
romantic drama and the classic drama
of our national theatre.

*His opinion
of Schiller
and the
romantic
drama.*

The question (says he) is not whether, by
bringing Schiller's dramas under certain rules,
and, comparing them with certain dramatic
forms to which we are accustomed, we find
them good or bad ; such a critical examination would be a superfluous and barren task.
But there may be advantage in finding out
what relations the works of Schiller bear to
their author, his character, position, opinions,
and the circumstances which surrounded
him. Such criticism is not perhaps so ready
and so absolute as that which praises or
condemns merely according to resemblance,
more or less, with given models ; but it belongs to the large study of mankind in
general, and that close observation of the progress of the human mind, which is at once the
most curious and most useful of all researches.

This was the new method which M. de Barante applied to the examination and appreciation of the romantic drama : but his criticism was neither narrow nor exclusive ; his admiration of Shakspere and Schiller did not chill his appreciation of Corneille and Racine ; nor while he gave full justice and fair homage to foreign works, did he cease to understand and enjoy our national literature. He ends his " Life of Schiller " with these liberal and judicious words :—

Doubtless it was the victorious sway of the French, added to his remembrance of the literary oppression from which Germany had freed herself, which gave Schiller those blind, narrow prejudices that he maintained to the last against our literature. There was in Germany a gathering up of declamatory commonplaces against our drama and our poetry in general, in which even the most distinguished writers joined. Philosophical criticism, general principles, and impartial acuteness never passed the Rhine. We were outlawed beyond the pale of literary justice

as completely, and as frivolously, as we ourselves outlawed the Germans; which in them
was more surprising and reprehensible, because we, at least, had judged them without
knowing them.

His creed concerning historical writing. M. de Barante's *Histoire des Ducs
de Bourgogne* is written from a more
special point of view, and in a more
systematic manner, though not so much
so as is sometimes said. He took for
the motto of his book Quintilian's maxim,
'Historia scribitur ad narrandum, non ad
probandum" ('History is written for nar-
ration, nor for demonstration'). All that
he thereby meant was, that history should
not be, like parliamentary or forensic
eloquence, a special pleading in favour
of a certain cause — a demonstration
founded on some preconceived opinion
or resolution. He never thought of
excluding from it the definitive judg-
ments and general principles which
legitimately spring out of historical facts,

and are their natural result. Facts ought
to be the basis and the groundwork of
history, while materialistic exactitude and
moral verity of relation, correct drawing
and life-like colouring, should be the
supreme end and aim of the historian.
These are self-evident axioms, which
M. de Barante accepted and believed as
sincerely as any one else; but he had also
observed and tested the spirit of the times:

We are (said he) in an epoch of doubt.
Absolute opinions have been torn from their
roots. Systems and criticisms are no longer
expected of the historian ; people are weary
of seeing him, like a pledged and docile
sophist, lend himself to any evidence which
any one chooses to extract from the past.
What is wanted, are facts, collected carefully
and brought vividly before our eyes ; then let
each man judge of them as he pleases—or
even let him form no precise opinion at all.
For there is nothing so impartial as imagination. She gives no definite dictum ; let but a
truthful picture be placed before her, and she
is satisfied.

The modern historian.

H

　　But lest these latter words should be misjudged, and in order better to explain the sense in which he uses them, M. de Barante adds :—

The duty of the modern historian.　　History, thus written, when the facts are presented with clearness and in fit order, and the historian is careful to choose those facts which best explain the period, should suggest to the reader reflections and comments which the author was unwilling to express. Therefore, I trust that, without having treated it explicitly, I have not ignored the vast question which occupies and absorbs all minds, and which is argued, either by words or blows, all over the civilized world ;—the question which in our day embraces politics, morality, religion, and even common human brotherhood ; —the war between power and freedom, might and right. If the histories which I bring before my reader's eyes shall make him feel how much a larger proportion of intelligence, common-sense, sympathy and equality between man and man, has improved, not only the arts and adornments of life, but the order of society, the morality of individuals, the sentiment of duty and religion ;—if I have convinced him that in spite of all vicissitudes and calamities, a civilized people may compare themselves with a just pride to their ancestors, who were bowed under such heavy yokes, and restrained by so many fetters, then, I believe, my labour will not have been thrown away. Studied in isolated portions, history may teach perversity or indifference ; we may see there violence, stratagem, corruption, justified by success. But regarded as a whole, and from a high point of view, the history of the human race has always a moral aspect ; for it demonstrates without ceasing that Providence, which, having put into man's nature the necessity and the capacity for self-improvement, allows no succession of events to make him doubt for one instant the reality of the blessing which has been given him.

M. de Barante was right thus to trust in the ultimate success of his book. No historian has ever abstained more completely from general reflections, philosophic notions, explicit and peremptory opinions ; or more exclusively confined

His " Histoire des Ducs de Bourgogne."

himself to the statement of facts gathered from original sources, and placed in their entirety before the reader's eyes. In truth, he seems only to have proposed to himself a sort of resurrection, dramatic and anecdotical, of the events which he records, and the persons who played their parts therein. Yet no historical work paints more faithfully the condition of France, its manners and its destiny, towards the end of the fourteenth and the beginning of the fifteenth century ; and no writer has made us better understand the absolute necessity of a more general civilization, of a social order more equitable, and of a government both more systematic and more free, if the external greatness and internal happiness of the French nation was to be secured.

The rapid success of the " History of the Dukes of Burgundy" showed with what a lively interest it inspired the public : published periodically in successive instalments between 1824 and 1828, in 1835 it had reached its sixth edition.

1827.

This was not M. de Barante's sole historical labour during the ten years between 1820 and 1830. In concert with me he took an active part in editing the *Revue Française*, a magazine which lived from January, 1828, to July, 1830. To it he contributed many articles on recent publications relating to the history of France in the seventeenth and eighteenth centuries. He was then projecting a work more important even than his "History of the Dukes of Burgundy;" it was the "History of the Parliament of Paris." In his letters to me at this time, I find traces of his thoughts and preparatory studies concerning it. On June 19, 1827, he writes :—

His successive works.

His "History of the Parliament of Paris."

I am reading up a little for data concerning the thirteenth century, and I am becoming a Royalist, like a Frenchman of the olden time. It is true justice increasing, and false justice diminishing ; order growing up by degrees in the sole quarter which contains some elements of it. If my opinions are not modified as I read on—which is just possible—I certainly shall not fall into the angers and lamentations of Boulainvilliers, Montlosier, and Sismondi over the civilians ; since parliament became not the king's court, but the court of the country gentleman. The whole institution seems to me to have had at first, and habitually, no character of centrality. I require, however, to examine this by the light of accurate evidence.

On the 10th of July following :—

His difficulties in the work.

I am plunging deeper and deeper into my work ; but I still cannot get my ideas fixed and clear. The documents are so scattered, that the whole matter becomes a sort of hypothesis, in which one must decide hastily on nothing. At first sight, it appeared to me that parliament was created by degrees, and was not substituted for any other court ; there was no such thing as a court of peers and barons, becoming afterwards an assembly of the commonalty. The more one advances, the more one finds traces of a sort of privy council, which gradually takes a judicial character. I cannot see that it was Philippe le Bel, who, as Pasquier alleged, first instituted the sittings of parliament, and settled its general form. All this beginning will cost me a deal of trouble, and I am so afraid of making mistakes.

On the 29th of August, after having heard of the formation of the Polignac cabinet, he thus writes :—

I have been quite turned aside from my own parliamentary work, and there was little need of any change of ministry to effect that. I read Mabillon, Baluze ; I make endless researches, and take innumerable notes—yet I do not begin anything. Still I am unwilling to make the book a work of controversy ; and after having formed an opinion I will assume no credit for the pains I shall have taken in reading up for it. I often investigate perfectly useless things ; but in order to know one point thoroughly, one should be acquainted with all its surroundings.

On the 19th of June, 1828, M. de Barante was elected member of the French Academy, in the place of M.

His election into the Academy.

de Sèze, who had died the 2d of May preceding. On the 20th of November he gave his inaugural discourse.

This was a difficult task. The one courageous act which had so justly made illustrious the name of M. de Sèze, was greater than anything else in his life or his writings. It was fitting to maintain, in his high place, the brave defender of Louis XVI., and yet not fall into ecstacies about his talent as an advocate. M. de Chateaubriand had just pronounced in the Chamber of Peers his *Eloge* on M. de Sèze; and though this *vivâ voce* oration only showed here and there traces of his brilliant written eloquence, still the comparison was dangerous. But M. de Barante comported himself worthily in a difficult

His Eloge upon M. de Sèze. position. His speech was grave and tender; high-toned, without being over-emphatic; on a level with the momentous memories it recalled, without any exaggerated effort to revive beyond due measure the impressions which it must naturally awaken, and which in truth it did awaken, thirty-five years after that hateful yet sublime tragedy had been enacted.

While devoting himself to this busy and fruitful literary life, M. de Barante also pursued in the Chamber of Peers the steady course of his political career—as candid, judicious, and moderate in the ranks of the Opposition as he had been when he was in power. All the great questions then in debate, and the important measures brought forward—such as laws concerning recruiting, sacrilege, succession, primogeniture, the war in Spain, the indemnity for emigrants, new enactments about elections and the press,—all these furnished him with opportunities for reports and speeches, which bore the same character of impartial independence, the same fidelity to general prin-

His conduct in the Chamber of Peers.

ciples and to moral equity, and the same political acuteness in applying them to the circumstances of the time. Still, beneath his severe and reserved language, there is often visible great depth of sadness. At this time he both thought and spoke like a man who feels that the political vessel in which he has embarked, and the well-being of which he sincerely desires, is drifting on, from error to error, towards some unknown abyss. I find this impression more clear and vivid than ever, in the letters which he wrote to me after the formation of the Polignac ministry.

A strange cabinet! (says he, on the 29th of August, 1829). They could hardly stand upon a smaller footing. Perhaps they will not wait even for the session, before throwing themselves into the open violation of law. Of their having a majority in the Chamber, I see no hope. Continually I incline to believe that whenever and however shall occur the moment of submitting, not negatively but

positively, to the yoke of the charter, they
will become capable of the maddest rashness.
Hitherto it does not appear that their old
party urges them on at all, but remains quiet,
in the provinces ; and to tell the truth, nobody
seems much excited on the matter.   We shall
see what will be done about the partial
election of next month.

Two months later, on the 22d of October, 1829, M. de Barante's uneasiness
was far greater; but it was as much
on account of the state of feeling of the
country as that of Charles X. and his
cabinet.

I fear this ministry will not be difficult to
overthrow ; and what will be done after its
fall I cannot conceive.   I feel a deep anxiety,
which is not dissipated by my knowledge of
the forces of the country.   If these forces do
not produce an effect purely comminatory,
if they manifest themselves in an active form,
I shall consider all our progress seriously
compromised.

It was impossible to foresee more
clearly the probable errors of both sides,

and the grave nature of their results. The revolution of 1830 was for M. de Barante no more than the confirmation of this double presentiment; he took no part in it, direct or active, but he unhesitatingly recognised its necessity; and when it was accomplished, he, in conjunction with his political friends of divers shades of opinion, from the Duc de Broglie and myself, to M. Molé, gave to the new monarchy his firm adhesion and loyal concurrence.

He then entered upon the career which, from his youth, his mother's tender ambition had most desired for him, and which he did not quit until his final secession from public life.

He is appointed ambassador to Turin.

On the 28th of October, 1830, he was appointed ambassador to Turin—a post which, for three centuries, had been in French political life a post more important than great; which he retained until, in September, 1835, he quitted it

for another more great than important—
that of ambassador to St. Petersburg.
So it was at the two courts most opposed to the government of Louis
Philippe that he was called upon to
represent it, and to serve it. The court
of Turin, by its Legitimist and Abso-
lutist traditions, and by its intimate relations with Austria, had, in spite of
its customary reserve and fluctuations,
vowed enmity and distrust towards the
régime which had resulted from the
revolution of 1830; while the Emperor
Nicholas, in a whim of pride and de-
spotic alarm, as obstinate as it was ill-
considered, had set himself in a relation, both embarrassing and malevolent,
towards the new constitutional King of
France. Consequently, M. de Barante,
during his two embassies to Turin and St.
Petersburg, had no political ties to form,
no important negotiations to carry out,
between his own government and these

two courts. To maintain with them, in spite of all the difficulties of the temper they were in, regular relations, as pacific as dignified—this was, in fact, all he had to do; and he acquitted himself of his mission with the prevision and ability of a mind remarkably just, delicate, full of tact, and with the tranquil vigilance of a temperament at once lofty and reserved.

His conduct at Turin. I will only cite from his diplomatic correspondence of this time a few instances, which show on one hand the constant propriety of his attitude towards the foreign powers, and on the other his keen penetration and the accuracy of the information which he transmitted to his own Government concerning the dispositions and views of those among whom he resided.

A short time after his arrival at Turin, in the midst of the festivities in celebration of the marriage of the Prin-

cess Marianna, niece of King Charles
Felix, to the King of Hungary, he wrote
thus—January 29, 1831—to General
Sebastiani, then Minister of Foreign
Affairs :—

The greatest novelty of the week is a ball
given by the nobility to the citizens of Turin.
In France, the mere idea of such an assembly
would once have implied, and would even
yet imply, irritating differences and divisions
to which general opinion is opposed, and
which good manners are slowly effacing. I
am not convinced that the commonalty of
Turin takes kindly to the nobility on account
of their rather haughty politeness ; but the
intention was sincere, and the general effect
seems to have been good. The entertainment was lively ; classes mingled thoroughly
and naturally. Among toilettes, indeed, the
spirit of equality was complete ; the higher
ranks were no better dressed than the lower.
The King was present ; the Princess de
Carignan danced, and I heard most aristocratic persons regret that she only took men
of birth for her partners. The Dowager-
Queen, Maria Theresa, was blamed for not

having allowed her daughter to dance. In short, this necessity for coaxing and honouring the middle classes—the feeling, more or less instinctive, that there must be found some transitionary means for passing into a new state of society—has singularly struck me. Some of these days the citizens are to return the entertainment of the nobility.

By the side of this instinctive labour of social innovation, M. de Barante was equally struck with the spirit of conservatism — immobility — in the relations between the Piedmontese upper and lower classes. Three months after the January fêtes King Charles Felix was dead, and King Charles Albert had ascended the throne. M. de Barante writes thus to General Sebastiani :—

Death of King Charles Felix.

I can show your Excellency by an amusing example to what point is carried here the respect for *statù quo.*

The theatre belongs to the palace. The king furnishes a subsidy for the undertaking. When people go to the opera they are said to

1832.

*His criti-
cisms on
social
customs
at Turin.*

be 'visiting the king.' Consequently, his Majesty distributes the boxes. The Manager receives the money for them ; but it is, in fact, a matter of court favour and aristocratic privilege. No citizen could get permission to hire a box ; even the magistracy and the second rank of the nobility have to content themselves with half boxes, in the upper tiers. What a grand subject for petty intrigues, jealousies, and vanities ! The restoration reestablished this offensive custom; and each year, at the beginning of winter, it is the cause of discontent and murmurings, often louder than for far more important things.

The late king's greatest pleasure was the theatre ; he never missed a night, and all this squabbling over boxes occupied him and amused him. But the king, Charles Albert, is different ; he hates the play-house—will scarcely put his foot into it. Nothing could suit worse with his grave temperament than to be mixed up with such things, so silly in themselves, so condemned by all sensible people, and also giving occasion for wounding the feelings of so many people, and exciting the spirit of jealousy between the nobility and the *bourgeoisie.* Nevertheless, in his fear of innovation, and his dislike to concede in any

I

way to the revolutionary spirit of the age, Charles Albert goes on distributing boxes like his predecessor.

Had Piedmont been a small isolated state, its petty internal and social agitations would have mattered little, and M. de Barante would scarcely have noticed them : but it was, for us French, the head of Italy ; and the destiny of the entire country, and the position of France therein with relation to Austria, were questions debated continually at Turin. Shortly after his arrival there, in order fully to acquaint himself with the state of matters, and give a clear account of the same, M. de Barante took a trip to Milan.

He visits Milan.

Milan (he writes to General Sebastiani) presents a very striking aspect, and if I had not gone there myself, no evidence that I could have received would have given me an idea of the condition of things. All that has been said of the Italian antipathy to

Austria comes far below the truth. It is the
most complete separation that can be imagined.
I have seen Paris occupied by foreign armies,
a remarkable sight, but nothing compared to
what one sees at Milan. It is not only the
middle and lower classes who manifest this
repugnance and distantness; there is not a
man in Milan whose hatred to the Austrian
government has been lessened by any marks
of favour shown to himself or his family.

The aristocracy, although made a great
deal of, and decorated with orders, and court-
levées, is as strongly national as the populace.
At a grand dinner given by the Conte Borromeo, General Zichy happened to be placed
next to the Contessa Vitaliano Borromeo,
daughter-in-law of the host. Towards the end
of the dinner, General Zichy, drinking a glass
of champagne, said that "he hoped soon to
be drinking it continually in France." "Certainly," replied the Contessa, "the French
are so hospitable, that they are sure to treat
their prisoners to their very best."

At this, General Zichy, either from his
national brutality, or because he had already
drank more wine than was advisable, and
having neither the tact nor good taste to
return jestingly a young girl's jest, broke

out into a fury. He said he was well aware of the bad feeling of the Milanese, their love of the French, and their hatred of the Austrians.

" If ever we have to quit Milan," added he, " I will console myself beforehand by shooting at least thirty Milanese."

Thereupon the Conte Vitaliano declared to his father, that whenever General Zichy was invited to the Borromeo palace, he and his wife would immediately quit it.

This scene was transacted at the house of the highest of the Milanese nobles, whom the Emperor of Austria had favoured more than any other, had made Chevalier of the Golden Fleece, and delegate for conducting home the Queen of Hungary; his son, this same Conte Vitaliano, bearing the title of Chamberlain to the Emperor.

The state of feeling in Northern Italy. The question is, with these strong feelings on the subject of Austria, are there united any definite projects? I cannot tell. The public opinion which gives force to conspiracy is one thing; actual conspiracy is another. Many who abhor the Austrians justly dread the convulsions and calamities of revolutionary war. These are the people who place all their hopes in us French; who wait for our inter-

ference, and implore from us their safety and
deliverance.

Such a state of feeling in Northern
Italy rendered the position of the
French ambassador at Turin singularly
difficult. He was the representative of
a policy at once liberal and anti-revolu-
tionary—basing itself upon patient ad-
vance and progressive order, national
independence and the peace of Europe.
The Government of 1830 had had the
courage to raise aloft this standard—
opposed to all popular passions, fiery
ambitions, and extreme party spirit of
every kind; and had borne it faithfully
in external as well as internal relations;
in its diplomatic intercourse with foreign
Governments, as in its public language
to the people themselves. It had thus
deprived itself of two engines of power
much in use among human affairs—
flattery and charlatanry, indecision and
duplicity; and had condemned itself to

*The policy
of the
French
Govern-
ment.*

hope much—a little too much—from the common sense, the moral sense, and the generally understood interest of mankind.

His complicated duties. This policy M. de Barante had to express and to carry out, in the face of the most opposite parties and their schemes, before the court of Turin and the Italian patriots, the Conservatives and the Liberals. He had to soothe the alarms of the one side and win the sympathies of the other; to disquiet or to reassure them; to satisfy each in turn by loyally and honestly making them acquainted with all they had to hope or to fear from the French Government in the different circumstances which might occur. Of this complicated duty he acquitted himself with intelligent candour. He kept his own Government carefully informed of the state of feeling of the divers Piedmontese parties, and communicated

faithfully to the Piedmontese the intentions of the French Government. On
the 10th of February, 1831, he writes
thus to General Sebastiani :—

You have often conversed with me on the
part Austria plays in this country, and the
possibility of a military intervention being
demanded or consented to by the Sardinian
Cabinet ; but we were arguing about an event
which had no actual probability. Now, things
are different. True, Piedmont is tranquil, and
Austria is not likely to increase her difficulty
by an invasion there ; but from day to day
what passes at Modena and Bologna may be
felt by a rebound at Genoa ; and even here, I
think I am justified by your words, and by
the general policy of our Government, in de-
claring that we shall hold all armed intervention on the part of Austria as a rupture
of treaties ; and shall, therefore, act as our
honour and interest demand. In truth, I do
not see how an ambassador of France can act
differently, in the present state of public feeling. Otherwise, all the impression of strength
and greatness made by the revolution of July
would be effaced, and there would be a
haughty triumph of all the opinions most

hostile to our country and her principles. We should be no longer feared, respected, or regarded.

On the morrow, the 11th of February, he thus writes :—

The principle of non-intervention.

By force of pressure upon M. le Comte de la Tour,* whom I see at least once daily, in order to ask of him Italian news, and to talk with him more than, I think, he quite approves of, I have arrived at a clearer notion of the present relations between the Sardinian Cabinet and Austria. I was once expressing to him my fears that Austrian intervention in Italy would produce grave results.

" But," said he, " France professes no absolute principle on this point. She admits that special motives and close neighbourhood might be a reason for intervention. Austria has taken, with regard to Italy, exceptions which have been admitted."

" I am not aware of it," answered I, " but I can warrant that nothing like this has been said or written to me concerning Italy. I am justified in concluding that, with regard to

* The then Minister of Foreign Affairs at the Court of Turin.

your country, we shall yield in nothing the
principle of non-intervention, and I can say
the same for the kingdom of Naples."

" Perhaps for Naples," said M. de la Tour ;
" Naples is a throne of the Bourbons."

" A motive which has little weight in present
politics. Naples and Sardinia are alike in the
eyes of France."

" Nevertheless," replied M. de la Tour, " I
am almost certain that in a conversation between Count Sebastiani and M. Appony,
Savoy was taken as an example of intervention justified by neighbourhood."

" Do you mean to say that Austria may
intervene for Piedmont, and we for Savoy ?
That would be too serious and too novel an
idea for my government to leave me in
ignorance of. We regard the kingdom of Sardinia as an individual and independent state,
not divided between the patronage of France
and Austria."

We went on from one thing to another,
though still keeping very moderate. However, M. de la Tour ended by saying to me—

" Intervention always resolves itself into a
question of fact. We intervene when we
believe it indispensable ; when we are strong
enough to do it, and when our intervention is

required. A war is better than a revolution ; the one has some favourable chances, the other has none."

We were now getting to something more positive.

" But," continued M. de la Tour, (I extract these significant words from a very long conversation,) " may God preserve us from all interventions ! We have them not now—we may never have need of them. In my opinion we had no need of them in 1821. We have an excellent army. We may maintain or reestablish good order at home. The King wishes no intervention ; it would displease him much. We must try everything else before having recourse to it, and our young Prince is both bold and decided."

For myself, I always took my ground upon the same text, which came back to me under all manner of aspects, and M. de la Tour and I parted on excellent terms, as usual.

*His con-
clusions
from the
conversa-
tion.*

But from all this, combined with what I have otherwise noticed, I must conclude that Austria, even before the troubles of Modena and Bologna, which she foresaw and could not prevent, has again pressed the Court of Turin to enter into some engagement—the answer to which has been that Turin does not

1831.

want her, and can do better without her help ;
but to this reply has been added a promise,
more or less formal, to make no concessions
either popular or constitutional, and to accept
intervention rather than consent to anything
of the sort. I think the Prince de Carignan
has, on his own account, entered into a similar
engagement.

Those who know the Prince well, and are
really attached to him, declare that he has
shown from his earliest youth a generous disposition, true high-mindedness, and a sincere
and warm desire for his country's good ; but
that the circumstances in which he found
himself during the troubles of 1821, the public
opinion—which he believes unjust—that was
then formed of him, and the position in which
he is here placed—distrusted by one party, and
unsupported by the confidence of the other—
together with his general relations towards
the King and Court; all these things have
given him a distaste for everything and everybody, withered up his nature, and left him a
prey to the *ennui* and ill-humour which appear to overwhelm him. I am informed that
late events in France, finding him in such an
unpropitious temper, have been criticised by
him with great bitterness. It is added that

His opinion of the Prince de Carignan.

on this occasion he assured the King that his Majesty might count on his, the Prince de Carignan's devotion, if ever the royal authority were attacked. Thus, whether this is really his feeling, or whether moral activity has diminished in him, we can by no means reckon that on his accession he will listen to the counsels of reform, even if there be no question of the charter, and a representative government. He will inherit, pure and simple, the inert rule of his predecessor.

Accession of King Charles Albert.

Three months after M. de Barante had written this letter, the Prince de Carignan was King Charles Albert.

Events pressed on in Italy. Insurrections broke out at Modena, Parma, Bologna; the Austrians intervened, drew back, retired; then intervened anew, to suppress a new revolt. The French Government maintained with credit the course of conduct which, from the first, it had declared it should adopt. We occupied Ancona—a proceeding counselled and warmly approved by M. de Barante. French influence, without overstepping the principles of our general policy, was visibly increasing in Italy, but was more than ever feared and repulsed by the Court of Turin.

On the 10th of October, 1832, M. de Barante wrote to Count Sebastiani :—

His criticisms on Charles Albert.

I must go back with more detail to the disposition of King Charles Albert, and his present scheme of government. I have, for this year past, explained to your Excellency how he has gradually given, I will not say confidence, that is a word which does not apply to the King of Sardinia, but credit to the whole Church party. It is passionately hostile to our government ; it monopolises almost all posts here, and in the diplomatic body it has two most devoted auxiliaries. M. de la Tour, both by his surroundings, his opinions, and his old associations, belongs properly to this party ; but he is a man so prudent, and so opposite to anything like decision or action, that he rather hinders than serves these ardent folk.

They are none the less in possession of the dominant influence at Court ; yet one cannot say that Charles Albert has yielded blindly to it. He sees therein his real safety ; he has started on this track, and he follows it, not finding in himself either will or conviction strong enough to lead him out of it : but he has no illusions, and no real liking for this class of opinions. In his private circle and private conversations—and he has no other— he allows any criticisms on the party he favours, the men he employs—even his own ministers ; nay, he goes beyond the remarks that are made to him, so much so that I have often seen the persons who were about him quite convinced that he was going to change his mode of action. But he has no real intention of the kind ; it is with him not pliability, only indecision of character. At bottom he is without any conviction of any kind. Devoid of active malevolence, having no pleasure in afflicting anybody, he yet knows not the meaning of confidence, affection, attachment. He dislikes and despises mankind, and loves disparaging conversations on the subject. As to principles, he has no longer any faith in them ; he applies a sort of discouraging contempt to everything and everybody ; ten years spent in constraint and dissimulation have accustomed him neither to take pleasure in actions nor to hold faithfully to convictions.

Such is Charles Albert in his relations with France. He has the most sincere desire to be at peace with us; the idea of war terrifies him, and with reason, for he sees in it the danger both of invasion and revolution. Certain ideas of enlarging his dominions, of attaining to the kingdom of Italy, have occupied his imagination; though grown dimmer, they are not yet dissipated; they may become hopes which will lead him to rest on our friendship. He spent his youth in France; he is well known there, and he wishes to keep up his good name; all that is done amongst us arrests his attention, and is almost his principal interest. At the same time he regards with visible rancour the revolution of July, which is in his eyes an affront and a danger to all royal races. He lives in fear, not only of propagandism, but of all liberal ideas; our newspapers and our parliamentary orators alike irritate and displease him. Not to clash against us, to risk no quarrels with us, and yet to hide every demonstration of good understanding, which is not quite indispensable,—such is the combination, more by chance than calculation, between his politics as a sovereign, and his personal impressions; added to which is his excessive self-love—

his love of rule, and his fear of being less a king than other monarchs, or of Sardinia being treated as an inferior sort of power.

It is hardly possible to analyse with more acuteness, or paint with more truth, the complicated character and variable nature of this prince : vowed at first to an obstinate although sceptical conservatism, and later in his reign, when chance seemed favourable to him, seized with a vast ambition, glorious in its contests and even in its defeats, until he fled suddenly from his throne and from society, to hide—and at last terminate—in a distant cloister, a life full of weariness, mad outbursts, discouragements, and mistakes.

For four years M. de Barante was a witness of this sad sight—this troubled spirit of a king—driven about by contradictory fancies which those about him could not fail to detect ; and during those four years the ambassador maintained,

1832.

in face of it all, the policy of his country, also very complicated, but candid and consistent; neither weakening it nor compromising it in anything, beyond the openly declared intentions of the French Government. No man could have been more naturally fitted for such a mission —which involved observation and conversation, rather than action; he comprehended his part as clearly as he practised it, and had no restless or self-conceited desire to go beyond it.

Under the date of March 21st, 1832, when the question as to what reforms should be brought into the Roman States was debated between the Court of Rome and the higher European powers, I find this letter from M. de Barante to General Sebastiani :—

His ideas concerning Italian Reform.

I had long intended to impart to your Excellency my decided opinion, that it was impossible to carry on at Rome, in the very seat of the Papal Government, any negotiation of which the result would be efficacious. M. de St. Aulaire informed me that such also was his opinion, and that it had long been held by your Excellency. The reasons which he can lay before you are doubtless much weightier than mine ; he sees for himself where I can only conjecture ; but he adds that he has indicated to your Excellency Florence or Turin as places where might be followed up advantageously a negotiation relating to pontifical affairs.

On this point I do not share his opinion. Florence, and even Turin, are too much within the influence of the Sacred College. The spirit which now animates the greater half of the Cardinals, and which forms the principal difficulty of the negotiation, is felt in every town of Italy ; and the party which is bound up with the oligarchy of the Roman Church would easily succeed in representing this question of policy and administration as a religious question. To have against us the opinion of the Court which we have fixed upon as the seat of negotiation, to throw the members of the conference in the midst of a society strongly opposed to the result which we wish to obtain, does not seem to me a happy combination.

1832.
Diplomatic negotiations.

I may add, that as regards Turin, there is here no diplomatic body capable of treating with so important a matter. I know not if your Excellency would consider me competent for such a mission; but I cannot see that the other ministers of foreign powers at the Sardinian Court would have enough importance or capacity for it to be confided to them. Obviously it would require men of enlightened judgment, liberal, and firm; and it is indispensable that they should have much weight and authority in the Cabinet which each represents.

I believe that this negotiation would be carried on better at Paris than anywhere else, only there must be obtained all possible local information. Everything should be collected that can throw light on the subject, and all questions must be pronounced upon with a complete knowledge of the present state of Italy.

It is seldom that in public affairs, even among the most honest functionaries, one finds such entire freedom from pretension or personal vanity; and so earnest an anxiety to penetrate to the root of things

He is appointed Ambassador to St. Petersburg.

and investigate all the chances of success or failure.

In September, 1835, the Duc de Broglie, who had lately become Minister of Foreign Affairs, had to make a great change in the French diplomatic corps. A personal knowledge of M. de Barante, and the trial which had been made at Turin of his impartial sagacity and quiet dignity, made it evident to the Duc that no better man could be chosen for the embassy to St. Petersburg. This mission, even more than that of Turin, was, for the Government of 1830, one of friendly attitude and attentive observation, rather than of direct and positive action. The feeling

The feeling of the Czar towards King Louis Philippe.

manifested, and the position assumed by the Emperor Nicholas towards the King, Louis Philippe, banished all idea of intimate relations and useful concord ; there was between France and Russia no national interest at stake—no weighty question pending. Since her reverses of 1831 Poland slumbered; the formation, already decided, of the kingdom of Greece, had made a pause in Eastern affairs; the Court of Russia did not mix itself up, as did that of Sardinia, in the troubles of its neighbour States. This embassy was an important post, but had few difficulties or embarrassments. There, one might watch things from a height, and regard them from a distance; but there was nothing to be done at the present, and nothing urgent to prepare against in the future. So M. de Barante was sent to St. Petersburg.

During the next six years—from 1835 to 1841—with the exception of rare intervals of absence, he resided constantly there, maintaining always the same attitude and the same language, and enjoying the same consideration which he had commanded from the first.

His attitude at St. Petersburg.

The Emperor Nicholas had little liking for foreigners, for clever men or men of independent spirit; but when they asked nothing of him, did not trouble him, and observed towards him a respectful reserve, he took some pleasure in having them about him as an ornament to his court, which, for a European court, was rather an original one. The " Memoirs of Madame de la Roche-Jacquelein," and the " History of the Dukes of Burgundy," had gained for M. de Barante widely extended literary fame : his conduct as ambassador at Turin showed him to be a tranquil and loyal diplomatist : his conversation was pleasing, and his character inspired confidence.

The Embassy and its difficulties.

His sojourn at St. Petersburg fully justified our hope in sending him thither, and the idea which had been formed of him in Russia on his arrival. Never, perhaps, was so important an embassy so chilling in all its relations, and so empty of events—yet nevertheless so fitly filled, thanks to the well-balanced tact, the calm and penetrating intellect, and the courteous yet gentle dignity of the ambassador. Two or three fragments of his correspondence, which I take from the beginning and the close of his residence in Russia, suffice to indicate both the character and the merit of the attitude he maintained in the delicate and yet hopelessly barren position in which he found himself.

On the 12th of January, 1836, he writes to the Duc de Broglie :—

The day before yesterday I presented my credentials to the Emperor. I was conducted to the palace, and introduced there with all the etiquette which is practised on similar occasions. I had intended, in giving his Majesty my letters, to address to him a few words, not wholly, but still partly official : however, he received me in his cabinet quite alone. Scarcely had I entered than I found myself close beside him, and he addressing

His first interview with the Czar Nicholas.

me with a courteous familiarity ; nay, talking with a sort of volubility, easy and elegant, which left no room for the formalities that I had meant to address to him.

Conversation began with a few personal compliments; the Emperor being convinced he had seen me in Paris,—which was quite impossible.   Then he spoke to me of the various posts I had filled,—of my *préfecture* in the Vendée, my various missions when I was *auditeur.*   He led the conversation whither he chose, and began speaking of diplomacy, which he said was not what it used to be.

"Now, everybody speaks out, and all are of the same mind.   All desire peace, for in it consists the happiness of Europe.   You have seen how Germany has profited by it, and how much she wishes its preservation : whatever people may think or say, it is just the same here.   Russia also has need of peace.

Within twenty years she has carried on four wars ; they have cost many millions, and what is far more to be regretted, the lives of three or four hundred thousand men.   It is time for us to occupy ourselves solely with the welfare of our people.   You see, I speak frankly ; I have no reserves ; my policy is strictly that of candour and loyalty."

As the Emperor spoke, he took my hand, and pressed it warmly, adding—

" People talk of war, but war is never made except out of necessity, or wilfulness. Of necessity there is none : nobody wants any-thing— there exists no cause for it, and no diffi-culty requiring it. And wilfully—neither I nor any other royal power would ever desire war."

All this was intermixed with a few words of my own. I leant stress upon whatever it seemed advisable to remark in the Emperor's words, and I tried to give things a turn which would best impart confidence in our French policy, and in our present position. Never-theless, I feared that this audience would slip by without his having said a word about the King (Louis Philippe), which would have been a serious matter. Nay, it seemed to me as if in order to escape the obligation of mentioning my sovereign the Emperor had given this informal character to our conversation, and made it a mere familiar chat.

The Czar's dislike of Louis Philippe.

I lay in wait for an opportunity. As I was holding my credentials in my hand, the Emperor took them from me, saying, "I must relieve you of these," and placed them on a table. I then said to him that in his kindness he had taken away from my presentation of them all character of etiquette, so that I had been unable to address to his Majesty any official language, or to convey to him the sentiments of my own monarch. My previous sentence had referred to the general desire for peace, so that the word 'sentiments' was obliged to be taken in its political meaning.

The Emperor extricated himself from his difficulty very cleverly and well. Without embarrassment or bitterness, but also without any pretence of kindly feeling, he spoke of King Louis Philippe,—of all that Europe owed him in the preservation of peace, of the difficult task he had undertaken, and the success he had obtained—of his capacity and wisdom. I tried to help out the Czar in every word, and to prolong as much as possible this

The Czar upon the attempt of Fieschi.

part of our conversation. Then he spake of the attempt of Fieschi in satisfactory terms ; with much horror at the deed, but with a depth of coldness likewise, referring neither to the King's calm courage, nor to what the Queen must have suffered : nothing in his words resembling the feeling I had heard expressed at Berlin. Then he added—

"This crime has opened all men's eyes,

and the position of things has consequently improved."

I spoke of the laws of September, and of their perfect conformity with the general opinion.

"Nevertheless, you require some others," said the Emperor, "and you will come to that yet."

"According to circumstances and public feeling," I replied. "In our form of government, and in our situation, we must wait until public opinion is forewarned and enlightened; then merit consists in profiting by the opportune moment."

In continuing this subject, he happened to say to me, allowing our very good position, "But will it last?"

I replied coldly, "There is no reason for any one to give himself on this head the slightest disquietude."

Nothing more was added in the matter.

After this Imperial conversation came others, with Count Nesselrode, Vice-Chancellor, and Minister of Foreign Affairs, M. Ouvaroff, Minister of Public Instruction, &c. Then ensued visits and invitations from the principal personages of the court. M. de Barante found them almost all disposed, and even anxious, to testify their disapprobation, or at least regret, at the attitude taken by the Emperor against King Louis Philippe; and these expressions became more frequent and more explicit the longer the ambassador remained at his post.

He wrote to me on this subject on the 28th of May, 1841 :—

The Czar's character, and the impossibility of influencing it. But in stating this fact to your Excellency and your predecessors, I have never ascribed to it any great importance. The Emperor's disposition resists all kinds of extraneous influence; he seldom listens to other people's ideas, and indeed scarcely takes them in unless they coincide with his own. Besides, no one attempts to change, or even to modify his convictions, less from fear of disgrace, than from the conviction that telling him the truth would be a useless labour, inasmuch as from the character of his mind, his opinions are absolute, and incapable of any variations. I speak especially of what relates to foreign politics, and the general concerns of Europe; for, in all that touches Russia and its internal government, its Emperor shows a remarkable mixture of wilfulness and prudence, despotism and good government.

When I perceived (he adds, on the 9th of February) that this hostile disposition towards France returned again and again in my various conversations with the Czar, I thought it advisable to speak of it indifferently and coldly, as a fact of which we were well aware, the consequences of which we did not exaggerate, and the longer or shorter duration of which was to us no great matter. I did not state this expressly, but the tone I took implied it, or something very like it.

In November, 1840, I had quitted my post as Ambassador to England; the Cabinet of October 29 had just been formed; and I was appointed Minister of Foreign Affairs. M. de Barante then wrote to me :—

Letters between himself and M. Guizot.

My dear Friend,—I am now under your orders, and in official correspondence with you, but I cease with regret our private one.—It appears to me that you and I shall find ourselves of one mind upon foreign as well as upon home politics. You undertake your task at a difficult moment. Could the actual position of affairs be averted ? You know much of which I know nothing ; if I am adequately informed respecting continental cabinets, I have no acquaintance with that of England, and still less with Lord Palmerston. You will certainly not find time to read the series of letters in which I tried to explain how and why Russia placed herself so eagerly at the disposal of Lord Palmerston, and agreed to all that England wished, and that we did not

His opinion of the Czar's intentions. wish. To break the alliance between France and England has been for ten years the fixed idea of the Emperor Nicholas. He long believed that this rupture would necessarily entail a European war, and in imagination he gave to himself the part of the Emperor Alexander, and the magnanimous head of the crusade against France. By degrees he saw that Austria and Prussia were by no means disposed to indulge him in this little pleasure, so that in urging on the treaty of last July, he did it without any ulterior notion of war. He only wished to satisfy his ill-will ; to place France in a bad position, and show us some affront. As to the East, he never thought of it : also the nation here cares less for conquest than Europe imagines ; it feels itself under too close surveillance. To send troops and ships to Constantinople was a thing more dreaded than desired, and people congratulated themselves sincerely in having escaped such perplexity and such expense.

When things began to grow embittered, and we were making great preparations, I think the idea of a European war returned, more or less, to his mind ; and that Vienna and Berlin were interrogated as to the state of quietness which Austria and Prussia maintained. The answer was of a soothing nature. Since then, the Emperor has lavished upon us the most pacific language, and deplored the misfortunes which war might bring on. Evidently, he does not wish—if things are settled—to be accused of having been more of a busybody and a stirrer up of war than his neighbours ; but this temper of his does not in the least imply that we should draw back from the course upon which we have entered. England may go as far as she likes, without hindrance ; if she wishes an arrangement with us, it shall be

willingly accepted, except for a little bad
humour, if our national honour is cautiously
treated. Russia would not promote this arrangement, as probably Austria and Prussia
will do ; but she would not put herself in
open opposition to it.

You will conclude from this, my dear
friend, that I have nothing to do here at St.
Petersburg. I look around me—I listen—and
that is all. In Russia, three distinct things
influence the course of politics : the opinions
or momentary impressions of the Emperor,
which are shown by indirect words, spoken
inconsequently, and not appertaining to his
official part at all. Nevertheless, there results
from them a general tone of popular feeling;
but it is modified, corrected, and guided by
the prudent and well-measured conduct of M.
de Nesselrode, who, on his part, is identified
with the cabinets of Vienna and Berlin, save
for his indifference upon certain points which
do not affect him much, such as Spain

*The Czar
the centre
of Russian
public
opinion.*

and Belgium. Finally, there is Russian
public opinion, which has no means of expressing itself, and no direct influence, but is,
nevertheless, the medium through which
government exists, and the atmosphere it
breathes. This public opinion never troubles

itself about European affairs, and would rather that the Czar did not do so; it has a decided kindness for France, and its only sore point in the West is Poland; in the East, the Dardanelles. . . . . . . You, my friend, will have need of courage and firmness, in which I am sure you will not be found wanting. If you terminate in a prompt and sufficiently honourable manner the question which now troubles France and disquiets Europe, you will, I believe, find a great and noble support in honest public opinion.

This letter fully confirmed me in the ideas I had formed in London on the feeling of the Emperor Nicholas towards us, the influence it had had upon the treaty of July, 1840, and the position in which we were placed towards Russia after this treaty. Before replying to M. de Barante, I waited until the debates upon the address from the two Chambers were ended, and the new Cabinet had a right to consider itself established. I thus wrote, in sending him the official de-

M. Guizot's letter to the Envoy.

L

spatch, which I addressed to our ministers
at different courts :—

*M. Guizot's
letter to M.
de Barante.*   I am just come out of a serious conflict.
The battle is, I trust, well won; but I do not
deceive myself about it—it is but the beginning of a long and rough campaign. Since
1836, after the fall of the Cabinet of October,
1832, the Government party has been virtually
dissolved, and Government itself is fluctuating,
humbled, weakened. Will the great peril into
which this road has led us, compel us to quit
the track? Shall we again seize upon the
benefits of a real and permanent majority in
consequence of the evils which its absence
has created? I hope so, and to this end I
shall labour unceasingly. My work has already commenced. The Chamber is cut in
two. Government has quitted its wavering
position between the centre and the left hand,
which has spoiled everything for four years;
but this is only a beginning. However, I do
not wish to convey to you my doubts and
anxieties; I believe success possible, in spite of
obstacles, perplexities, weariness, and checks
innumerable. This ought to suffice me, and
should suffice all wise men; the condition of
humanity allows of nothing easier.

1841.

M. Guizot's letter to M. de Barante.

As to external affairs, I can add little to my official despatch, wherein I trust I have explained clearly the attitude and the language I require of you ; for there is at present nothing more to be done than to assume a certain attitude, and use a certain language. Isolation is not a condition that one would deliberately choose, or in which one would remain for ever ; but when it exists one must live in it with tranquillity, until one can leave it with profit. A neutral position has now for us one great advantage—liberty. Ours is at this time perfect. We owe nobody anything. We are free from all rivalries, as from all pledges. We can look straight at the future. We have no intention of remaining strangers to the general affairs of Europe. We believe it is good for us, and for others, that this should not be; and we are certain of once more entering into the field. France is too great for the void of her absence not to be speedily felt. We await the time when this will be felt and said. I have an intense dislike for braggadocio, but tranquil expectations and freedom of choice are now best fitted for us.

I need not here repeat the story of the negotiations which brought on this

The Convention of July, 1841.

condition of things; elsewhere I have accurately and minutely detailed them.* Their result, as is well known, was the Convention of July, 1841, which put an end to the neutrality of France, and caused her to take her place once more in the common deliberation of the great Powers upon their relations with the Porte and with Western affairs, now become a subject of European consideration. This was not the abolition of the treaty of July, 1840, because it had, upon the question of Egypt, received its execution and attained its end; but it was the termination of the exceptional and dangerous position in which this treaty had placed both France and all Europe. Learning this termination, M. de Barante thus wrote to me :—

His receipt of the Convention, and its results at St. Petersburg.

The Lubeck packet-boat brought me yesterday the convention signed in London on the 13th instant, by the plenipotentiaries of

* In M. Guizot's *Mémoires pour servir à l'Histoire de mon Temps*, vol. vi. p. 37.

the Five Powers. M. de Nesselrode sent me also a copy, as well as the protocol of the 10th of July. His note accompanying them expressed the satisfaction which this good news had given him, and reminded me that the evening before he had announced to me that it could not be long in arriving. I took great care to show no *empressement*—no keen desire for our being reinstated in the deliberations of the Four Powers—lest M. de Nesselrode, showing me this courtesy, should think he was giving me a great pleasure, and putting an end to my impatient expectation: his note was a token of. his own satisfaction rather than of mine.

The effect has been similar in the diplomatic body. The Ministers of England and Prussia, and the Austrian *chargé d'affaires*, have all hastened to show me how much they rejoice in the fortunate concord between these Powers and France. I have no reason to suppose that the Emperor has received a contrary impression; it is a strong point in his character to wait with a sort of impatience for an event which is considered necessary, and in which he has made his decision. He has at least the satisfaction of having essentially contributed to this end—that the Egyptian

How the Czar received the news.

affair should be solved in a manner quite
opposed to the wishes of the King's government. To tell the truth, his views did not
extend beyond that; he never thought of
assuming the privilege of conquest, or of increasing the dangers and embarrassments of the
Ottoman Empire: he did not desire war—at
last he actually dreaded it; or at least he saw
that the German powers would avoid it at all
cost. He could only hope that French neutrality would last, and that we should have
less and less of influence in European affairs;
but for the last two months he has ceased to
reckon on this pleasure. So he is now accustomed to his new position, which began even
before his signing the Convention."

The Czar's annoyance.

M. de Barante had too much confidence in the good sense and resignation
of the Emperor Nicholas. In presence
of an obvious necessity, a despot will
succumb to his own helplessness, but
cannot forget his annoyance; and as soon
as an opportunity offers of manifesting
the latter without seriously compromising himself, he will hasten to seize

it. The Czar did not seize upon his opportunity; he created it. Three months after the signing of this Convention of July—on the 30th October, 1841—Count de Pahlen, Russian ambassador at Paris, came to see me, and read me a despatch dated the 12th, which he had just received from Count Nesselrode. Therein the Emperor regretted not being able to send for his envoy from Carlsbad to Warsaw, as he desired some conversation with him. If no important business required him in Paris, the Emperor demanded his presence in St. Petersburg, but named no definite time for his departure.

I asked no explanation, and Count de Pahlen offered none. He departed on the 11th of November following.

We could not, and did not, deceive ourselves as to the true motive of this imperial command, and of the ambassador's sudden departure. It was the

Diplomatic under-currents.

yearly custom that on New Year's Day, and the 1st of May, which was the fête-day of King Louis Philippe, the diplomatic circle should come, as well as the divers national authorities, to pay their respects to the King; and that the senior foreign ambassador should be the one to speak in the name of the rest. Many times this duty had fallen to the lot of the Russian envoy, who had discharged it without embarrassment, like the rest of his colleagues. On the 1st of May, 1834, and the 1st of January, 1835, Count Pozzo de Borgo had been the interpreter of their sentiments. In the autumn of 1841, Count d'Appony, then senior ambassador, happened to be away from Paris, and his absence extended over New Year's Day, so the Count de Pahlen, the next in seniority, would have had to replace him in the ceremonial. The Emperor Nicholas, still full of annoyance at the check he had received in his ill-will to the French Government, by the Convention of July, 1841, did not wish so immediately afterwards to allow his ambassador to pay a public homage to the wisdom and the undoubted position of King Louis Philippe. So he gave himself the paltry satisfaction of showing, by this sudden recal of Count Pahlen, the ill-temper which he had hitherto been careful to hide. .

This incident and its consequences are too well known for me to pause upon either; besides, I have already related everything in publishing the diplomatic documents.*

When the Russian ambassador quitted Paris, M. de Barante received three months' leave from St. Petersburg, and I gave immediate orders to the chief secretary of the French embassy there, M. Casimir Perier, his temporary

* In the *Mémoires pour servir à l'Histoire de mon Temps.*

substitute, to remain shut up in his hotel on the festival of St. Nicholas, and to allege indisposition as a reason for declining the invitation which he would doubtless receive from Count Nesselrode. This was repaying, simply but pointedly, to the Czar, the disrespect he had shown to King Louis Philippe ; and M. Casimir Perier executed my instructions with equal dignity and circumspection.

The Emperor's violent anger, the burthen of which he imposed upon his court by interdicting for several months all social relations with M. Casimir Perier and the French embassy, did not however pass beyond strict diplomatic courtesy. But from this day, though both still retained the title of ambassador, M. de Barante returned no more to St. Petersburg, nor Count Pahlen to Paris. From 1842 to 1848, in spite of some indications at St. Petersburg of a desire to put an end to the coldness subsisting between the two courts, our Cabinet maintained the position which it had taken, and between France and Russia there were only *chargés d'affaires.*

During these six years of involuntary idleness, M. de Barante did not remain inactive. When the Chamber of Peers was sitting, he took an assiduous share in its labours. He received much consideration in it, and was always ready to give to our Government useful support. Almost all the rest of the year he spent at his estate of Barante, occupying himself by turns with the local matters of his native region, and with establishments for instruction, public benefit, or Christian charity, which he had either founded or endowed.

Meantime he kept up with me an intimate correspondence, full of his own ideas and impressions—whether pleasant or mournful, trustful or apprehensive, upon the condition of France and its government; the Cabinet—my own position there; and the good or ill chances of the policy to which we were both of us pledged and devoted. At the approach of the session of 1843, when the shock of 1840 had well-nigh ceased, he thus wrote to me :—

The quietude which we enjoy continues yet, and seems to take a character more natural and less transitory. I never remember to have seen a time when there was so much repose in men's minds; and, I should say, so much security for the future. You may have to gird yourself for battle in three months, but every tranquil day gives you better chances. An Opposition which cannot tell what its points of attack shall be, sees, necessarily, its forces diminished. If you clear this session, you will have a high and fine position.

Three weeks later he was more struck with the permanent perils of the situation :—

There is, in the government of this country, one radical difficulty. It needs repose; it loves *statu quo*; it holds fast to its routines;

in the care of its interests there must be nothing hazardous or disturbing. While on the other side, people's minds like to be occupied and amused; their imaginations must not be left a prey to *ennui*; they remember the Revolution and the Empire. Of these two inclinations, the first is more real than the second. M. Thiers himself is not deceived on this point; at least his reason acknowledges it: I think I told you what he once wrote to me, that "what France needs is a ministry like that of Cardinal de Fleury."

You ought then to humble yourself to the patient pleasure, often without any credit, of throwing daily into the scale which you judge the best, a few grains of sand. Therefore, you will make no treaty concerning a tariff of customs duties with Belgium: you will decide on nothing in the East: your ministerial talent will consist in demonstrating to both Chambers, and to the public in general, that this is not your fault but theirs, and that no one else, no more than yourself, can succeed in urging them on to great undertakings.

A year later, after the visit of Queen Victoria to the Chateau d'Eu, and the decided re-establishment of friendly rela-

tions with England, his impression of
things became more hopeful :—

> You ought to be content (he wrote to me),
> for in truth the country seems so. Without
> doubt its present well-being gives it neither
> confidence, nor affection, nor gratitude ; it
> even sets itself on its guard against such
> sentiments ; but it is consciously ,calm, and
> congratulates itself in its repose. As you say,
> this is no guarantee for a quiet session ; the
> Chamber represents sufficiently the state of
> public opinion ; but it contains within itself
> other elements, — exacting self-interests,
> wounded self-love, rancour, ambition. All
> these may be combined, by intriguing *coteries*,
> in a perplexing manner. You have a good
> courage—that is one chance of victory. Like
> your neighbours, you love success and power ;
> but you have one thing more than they have—
> you do not fear trouble, you accept it as a
> necessity ; nay, it scarcely displeases you.

Thus M. de Barante was, for my sake,
a distant spectator of things, far-seeing,
judicious, cool ; and his correspondence
brought to me by turns prudent anxieties
or affectionate encouragements.

They who, in the labours and trials of active political life, expect to find many true friends, will be deceived. One must not even be too nice or too exacting with those upon whom one has a right to reckon ; they all have their own surrounding circumstances — private interests, future career, tastes, and fancies. The close and permanent union of mind and destinies is a joy and a strength that does not belong to public life ; which, nevertheless, is not without close ties and sincere attachments. That man would be unjust, as well as foolish, who could not both count its costs and gather up its advantages.

Less stormily for him than for me, but not the less completely, came the revolution of February, 1848, at once putting an end to the public life of M. de Barante, as well as to my own.

He felt that the new *régime* could offer to him nothing desirable, so he

1848.
Political friendships.

The Revolution of February. His political career ends.

retired permanently to Barante with his family. Not, however, renouncing the useful employment of his active intellect, or the moral service of his country; he resumed his labours as a historian, and a looker-on at political events. To this date belong some of his most important works of both kinds; of the first his *Histoires de la Convention Nationale et du Directoire Exécutif*, his *Vie Politique de M. Royer-Collard*, and the numerous biographical essays which, in 1858 and 1859, he collected in four volumes, and published under two titles, *Etudes Historiques et Biographiques*, and *Etudes Littéraires et Historiques*. But it is among politics, properly called—either the politics of theory or of events, that

His historical and political writings.

we may class his *Observations sur les Déclarations des droits de l'Homme et du Citoyen;* his *Réflexions sur les Œuvres Politiques le Jean-Jacques Rousseau*, and his *Questions Constitutionelles*, works first

published in 1849, and inserted afterwards. in the two collections which I have
named.

In considering merely these subjects
and titles, the historical labours of M.
de Barante possess, within their own
limits of French history exclusively, one
principal and striking characteristic—
extent and variety. He has travelled
over and retraced the most different
periods of our national existence : the
mediæval period, when near its end ;
the seventeenth century, in its splendour
and decline ; the eighteenth, during its
ambitious work of the decomposition and
the re-construction of French society :
the Revolution, the Empire, the Restoration, the Monarchy of 1830, in their
outbursts and essays.

In his portraits of the Dukes of
Burgundy, Louis XIV., the Regency,
Louis XVI., Mirabeau and Robespierre,
Napoleon, Louis XVIII., and Louis

M

Philippe, he has traced France through all her trials and transformations, to the beginning of that new social condition which she is still labouring to found. And besides this first characteristic— extent and variety--there appears in M. de Barante's writings a second, more rare still; free thought, and perfect equity, reign throughout all these recitals, these pictures of the most opposite times. The author contemplates and comprehends, as a spectator at once sympathetic and independent, ideas, manners, acts, far removed from the present state of things. Truth has for him such a powerful charm, that he delights to contemplate it in its most simple and authentic form.

But he does not stop there, contenting himself with erudite exactitude and fidelity of imagination. Beneath all this, and even when he appears to trouble himself only about surface painting, he intends, and he accomplishes, far better things. He has his own large idea of human society — of its institutions, governments, and the duties and rights of those connected with them, whether great or small, princes or peoples. This idea he allows to be clearly visible, from time to time, through his modest and exact recitals. He is, in truth, neither a philosopher nor a politician; he labours neither to establish a system nor to uphold a party; but he is a moralist as well as a historian. In his free and flexible course he yet has continually a torch to light him, a clue to guide him, a goal towards which he steadily moves on. If he reproduces men and their acts as in a mirror, their images are reflected by an intelligent and honest critic, who, by the mere attitude he takes, or by a few simple words, qualifies them according to good sense and justice.

M 2

How wise, for instance, is this line from Lucan, which M. de Barante takes as the motto of his *Histoire de la Convention Nationale* : " Jusque datum sceleri ; " ' Law in the hands of crime.' The most eloquent anathemas sink to nothing compared to this brief description of the Reign of Terror, and the most fanatical apotheoses of the period can never efface the sting of these words.

M. de Barante's political writings, both theoretical and practical ; his work *Sur les Communes et l'Aristocratie*, his *Réflexions sur les Œuvres Politiques de Jean-Jacques Rousseau ;* or, as he also entitled them, his *Histoire de l'Egalité en France ;* his *Questions Constitutionnelles*, or *Essais sur la Souveraineté, le Suffrage Universel, les emplois Publics, la Propriété, le Travail*, &c.—all these demonstrate the same qualities ; wide and liberal intellect, impartial equity, and moral strength.

His opinions are settled, yet are neither
obstinate nor exclusive ; he wishes to
respect the rights of all, but exacts from
all respect for rights ; he never sacrifices one principle to another, or one
interest to another ; he understands the
various and complicated elements which
exist in all human society, takes account
of the whole, and never loses sight of
the part which each individual requires
to play.

Therefore, he accepts the great social
problem in its fullest extent, though without renouncing the hope of solving it ; he
is a stranger to all indifferent and un-
steady scepticism, as he is to all narrow
and tyrannical dogmatism. He does not
admit that intelligent reason and practical good sense are in opposition, and
believes that order and freedom may
and ought to be reconciled, under diverse
forms and degrees, according to place
and time. He persists in following

trustfully the grand aim of nature and human nature, without ignoring the diversity and roughness of the paths that lead thither, and with a resigned acceptance of the slowness of the progress.

It is these noble characteristics which constitute M. de Barante one of the most faithful representatives of that great but modest party which I have called the party of good sense and moral feeling— so often misunderstood, beaten down, saddened, discouraged, yet unconquered still; invincibly persevering, both in aspiration and effort, in spite of all its misfortunes and reverses. Humanity has deep instincts, which are stronger than its bitterest trials, and which it obeys without recognising how much trouble must be taken, how much time there is to wait, before these instincts can be satisfied. Such is the condition of the party I have named : it is destined to suffer much, yet never to perish; it has at the core, in its own strong justice, more faith in itself than it takes credit for; it hopes on, even when it believes its case desperate; it works on, though seeming to renounce its labours. And if in one of its ill times it finds a man who is of its own sort, and who has devoted to it, not without some credit, his intellect and his whole career, immediately public sympathy wakes up, and follows this man even to his grave, in order to distinguish him from the common herd, and to honour him accordingly.

Herein I find the hidden cause the motive springing from instinct rather than reflection, but most real and decisive, of the feeling manifested at the death of M. de Barante, by the people who had witnessed his life, and even by the general public, who, from a distance, were well acquainted with his name and his writings.

1849-66.
The party to which he belonged.

Its homage to him at his death.

He died popular — recognised as a
sincere and faithful defender of ideas,
sentiments, interests, and hopes which
in France, and I may say throughout
Europe, still live in the hearts of wise
and good men, in spite of the struggles
of the present, and the dark clouds of
the future.

Did M. de Barante foresee the popu-
larity that would follow him in his grave,
and would he have attributed it to that
true and worthy public instinct which is,
in my view, its principal cause ? I doubt
this. While, up to his latest hour, he
maintained all his liberal and moral convictions, still he could not avoid having,
with regard to the actual state of men's
minds and acts in France, a feeling of
great sadness and uneasiness. It then
befell him, as it befals all chosen souls,
when the world refuses to give them
what they have hoped and desired,—
that he turned his eyes away from it,

and asked of God Himself that faith
and trust which it was essential to him
to have in the ultimate destiny of
humanity.

Precisely a year ago, I sent to M. de
Barante my *Méditations sur l'État actuel
de la Religion Chrétienne en France.*
He answered in a letter, the hand-
writing of which was already tremulous
and feeble :—

I thank you, my dear friend, for the book
which you have kindly sent me ; it is worthy
of yourself, and will do much good. The
eighteenth century lifted itself up against
religion ; the nineteenth doubts the very
existence of God. From the effect, people
must come to the cause. I am certain of
your success.

Religious ideas and sentiments—or, to
call things by their right names, the
hopes and beliefs of Christianity—had
become the constant and dominant
thought of M. de Barante. Already

he had begun to regard, as from afar off, the world and its concerns; keeping still the same affectionate interest in it, but viewing all things with the serenity of one who has come to breathe a higher and purer air. In this spirit, so noble and so lovely to behold, he quitted his household hearth, his wife, his children, all that he loved here below, and the country which he had faithfully served and honoured. That country, in its turn, owes both to itself and to him, to honour M. de Barante as one of the most distinguished and noble of her children.

AN ADDRESS,

DELIVERED AT THE GENERAL SITTING OF THE

HISTORICAL SOCIETY OF FRANCE,

May 7, 1867.

By M. GUIZOT, President.

AN ADDRESS.

GENTLEMEN,—You have done me an honour for which I am deeply grateful, yet it leaves me deeply sorrowful. Most honourable is it to be elected by your unanimous votes to replace M. de Barante, yet it is most sad thus to have to succeed a friend true and faithful, whose friendship for me has lasted more than half a century ;—this, during the crises and vicissitudes which, in our generation, have, practically and theoretically, so strongly agitated all men, both as nations and as individuals. When everything is tottering and changing around one, what a rare blessing is a firm, persistent friendship ! And the friendship which united M. de Barante and myself, drew its source from a cause which I can trace with satisfaction through the long series of years—a constant and close sympathy in our tastes, our labours, our principles, and our fortunes.

We both took a keen delight in literature and politics, between which we divided ourselves, and to which we wholly devoted our lives. And in this double career we were attached to the same kind of studies, and to the same good cause. In literature, history, and politics alike, the principle of free and constitutional government was the chosen object of all our thoughts and acts. When, in 1808, M. de Barante published his *Tableau de la Littérature Française au dix-huitième Siècle*, I was retracing the poetic literature of the seventeenth century—those *chefs d'œuvres* of Corneille which raised to so high a pitch the dramatic glory of our country; and when, in 1821, I translated Shakspere, my friend did the same for Schiller; nay, he assisted me in my own labours, for the translation of *Hamlet* is his work. Between 1820 and 1830, while I was devoting myself to the study of the origin and progress of French civilization, M. de Barante wrote his *Histoire des Ducs de Bourgogne*,

resuscitating in its vivid, natural form, one of
the grandest epochs of that series of centuries
which I was trying to explain by giving them in a
continuous view. And when, after the year 1830,
politics took the principal place in both our lives,
we both constantly upheld the same principles,
pursued the same end, and turn by turn gained the
same successes or underwent the same reverses.

Thus, gentlemen, I trust you will not be sur-
prised—nay, will pardon me—if I linger with pleasure on these tokens of the sympathy—I believe,
the perfect harmony—in which we lived together :
we, the two men whom you have successively
called to the honour of your presidentship. I take
a sad comfort in thus linking myself, as I near my
grave, with the friend who has already sunk before
me into his ; and my remembrances of our long
union are to me the most welcome explanation, as
doubtless they were to you the principal motive, of
your choice.

When, thirty-three years ago, gentlemen, you
elected M. de Barante president of your rising
Society, you judged accurately and clearly both the

character of his works and their suitability for
your ends. You wished to place before the
France of to-day, in a form correct and complete,
the principal records of historic France of old,
upon which our forefathers have left so strongly
the original impress of their daily lives, characters,
and destinies. You thought, with good reason,
that familiarity with these records would be, for
our modern France, a matter of both curiosity and
instruction.

It is the great honour and privilege of the race
of man—a privilege which it has received direct
from its Creator—that it alone possesses *a history*.
That is, we form one of a series of generations,
each the heir of all the others, and intimately
linked together by a general and permanent bond,
instead of being a mere succession of isolated
beings, who are ignored and forgotten as soon as
they pass away, turn by turn, from this mortal
earth. But in order that this sublime privilege of
ours should shine in all its brightness, and gather
up all its fruits, it is needful that the successive
generations of men should truly know and under-

stand one another. I say more : it is necessary
that they should bear towards each other an affectionate regard, and that every one, in freely choos-
ing what suits itself best out of the heritage of its
ancestors, should faithfully remember all that it
owes to them, and render unto them a grateful
justice.

This, gentlemen, is the precise sentiment which
so constantly animated M. de Barante in his historical studies. He ever presented before his reader
ancient as well as modern France. He knew both;
he understood, respected, and loved both, even as
it lay deep in his heart that sons should invariably
know, understand, respect, and love their fathers.
And ancient France has truly a right to be so
regarded by us moderns. Her destiny has been
stormy, diversified, incomplete ; she has sought
and attempted much more than she has ever
accomplished; she has been more fruitful than
fortunate, more brilliant than far-seeing. But she
has never lacked either genius, valour, power, or
glory ; and if she has not rapidly attained all the
conditions of national liberty and happiness, she

N

has constantly offered to the world many and rare
models of those noble qualities which, in the most
opposite walks of life, exalt and dignify mankind.

M. de Barante had been vividly struck with this
wonderful activity, this intellectual and moral
wealth, shown by ancient France in spite of all
her trials; and whether he found it in the heroic
adventures of the middle ages, the struggles of the
sixteenth century, the splendours of the seventeenth, or the ambitions of the eighteenth, he took
a noble delight in paying it homage, and in retracing all its merits as clearly as he did its errors
and its misfortunes.

But his large national sympathy was free from
all lengthy lingering over favourite reminiscences,
and pure from all prejudiced exclusiveness or obstinate adherence to class or party; and when he
had to pass from the France of old times to the
France of to-day, to relate the history and appreciate the work of the new state of society which,
after 1789, rebuilt itself so laboriously upon the
ruins of ancient France, he still maintained, both in
his mpressions and judgment of things, the same

patriotic instinct and independence of spirit, the same care and skill in dividing the good from the evil, and appreciating the former under its most variable aspects. He hoped everything for his country, and he flattered her in nothing.

His different historical writings may be put to a close test. We may place side by side his *Histoire des Ducs de Bourgogne* and his *Tableau de la Littérature Française au dix-huitième Siècle ;* his *Histoires de la Convention Nationale et du Directoire Exécutif* may be compared with his *Mémoires de Madame de la Roche-Jacquelein* and his *Vie de M. Royer-Collard*, and we shall find, between these records and critical appreciations of such diverse periods and events, neither dissonance nor contradiction. Everywhere there shines forth in his writings a filial and respectful love for France in all her various fortunes, and for every one of her illustrious children. Everywhere there reigns a clear moral perception, superior alike to illusions and subterfuges ; a lofty, yet supple political intelligence; an equity free from sceptical indifferentism ; and an unconquerable determination to deal justly with all, and to tell the truth, under all circumstances, concerning all.

I do speak, and must speak, here, solely of the historian : nevertheless I wish to give you a glimpse of the man himself.

M. de Barante was one of those men who are in earnest in everything they say and do ; who feel the strong need of having their principles and their lives continually in close accord. Thus, in defiance of all the complications and precipitate transformations of our time—whether it was his lot to speak or be silent, to act or abstain from acting, to enter or to quit the public arena—M. de Barante constantly obeyed the laws which he had laid down for himself, as a just and honest man, and a thinker well convinced of his opinions. In all matters and on all occasions, in politics as in literature, in religion as in politics, his faith governed his actions, and his actions bore testimony to his faith.

After not far short of a half-century of public life, he passed his last twenty years in dignified obscurity, beside his native hearth, in the bosom

of his family, faithful to his principles, his affections, and his remembrances of the past, solely
occupied in scattering among the people that surrounded him good works and good examples.
And worthily did his compatriots respond to this.
When he died, the whole country side hastened to
press around his grave, and his obsequies were a
grand and spontaneous homage paid by the land
where he was born, lived, and died, to his career
and his renown.

It was yours, gentlemen, and fitting for you, to
have chosen such a man for the honour of presid-
ing at your labours. He enjoyed it during thirty-
three years, as a just recompense for the services
which he had rendered to our country's history.
And now, since it pleases you to transfer this
honour from his head to mine, I will record here,
in justification of your choice, the words which
M. de Barante wrote himself in his last will and
testament :—

"*I will not end these pages, to which are confided
my latest thoughts, without naming the friends who
remain mine. I wish them to know how sweet their*

friendship has been to me, and I desire that they should not forget me when I am no more. It is my request that this testimony should be transmitted especially to M. le Duc de Broglie and to M. Guizot."

To this last expression of a friendship so faithful, I will add, gentlemen, only one word — a word that M. de Barante himself might take pleasure in hearing. His wish shall be accomplished : he shall not be forgotten.

THE END.

www.ingramcontent.com/pod-product-compliance
Lightning Source LLC
Chambersburg PA
CBHW022353020726
47500CB00002B/249